A Collection of
Robert Sheckley
Science Fiction

A Collection of
Robert Sheckley
Science Fiction

Printed in the United States of America and Australia.

The Gnome Press
www.TheGnomePress.com

ISBN: 978-1-61203-983-1

Content

BESIDE STILL WATERS

When people talk about getting away from it all, they are usually thinking about our great open spaces out west. But to science fiction writers, that would be practically in the heart of Times Square. When a man of the future wants solitude he picks a slab of rock floating in space four light years east of Andromeda. Here is a gentle little story about a man who sought the solitude of such a location. And who did he take along for company? None other than Charles the Robot.

Mark Rogers was a prospector, and he went to the asteroid belt looking for radioactives and rare metals. He searched for years, never finding much, hopping from fragment to fragment. After a time he settled on a slab of rock half a mile thick.

Rogers had been born old, and he didn't age much past a point. His face was white with the pallor of space, and his hands shook a little. He called his slab of rock Martha, after no girl he had ever known.

He made a little strike, enough to equip Martha with an air pump and a shack, a few tons of dirt and some water tanks, and a robot. Then he settled back and watched the stars.

The robot he bought was a standard-model all-around worker, with built-in memory and a thirty-word vocabulary. Mark added to that, bit by bit. He was something of a tinkerer, and he enjoyed adapting his environment to himself.

At first, all the robot could say was "Yes, sir," and "No, sir." He could state simple problems: "The air pump is laboring, sir." "The corn is budding, sir." He could perform a satisfactory salutation: "Good morning, sir."

Mark changed that. He eliminated the "sirs" from the robot's vocabulary; equality was the rule on Mark's hunk of rock. Then he dubbed the robot Charles, after a father he had never known.

As the years passed, the air pump began to labor a little as it converted the oxygen in the planetoid's rock into a breathable atmosphere. The air seeped into space, and the pump worked a little harder, supplying more.

The crops continued to grow on the tamed black dirt of the planetoid. Looking up, Mark could see the sheer blackness of the river of space, the floating points of the stars. Around him, under him, overhead, masses of rock drifted, and sometimes the starlight glinted from their black sides. Occasionally, Mark caught a glimpse of Mars or Jupiter. Once he thought he saw Earth.

Mark began to tape new responses into Charles. He added simple responses to cue words. When he said, "How does it look?" Charles would answer, "Oh, pretty good, I guess."

At first the answers were what Mark had been answering himself, in the long dialogue held over the years. But, slowly, he began to build a new personality into Charles.

Mark had always been suspicious and scornful of women. But for some reason he didn't tape the same suspicion into Charles. Charles' outlook was quite different.

"What do you think of girls?" Mark would ask, sitting on a packing case outside the shack, after the chores were done.

"Oh, I don't know. You have to find the right one." The robot would reply dutifully, repeating what had been put on its tape.

"I never saw a good one yet," Mark would say.

"Well, that's not fair. Perhaps you didn't look long enough. There's a girl in the world for every man."

"You're a romantic!" Mark would say scornfully. The robot would pause—a built-in pause—and chuckle a carefully constructed chuckle.

"I dreamed of a girl named Martha once," Charles would say. "Maybe if I would have looked, I would have found her."

And then it would be bedtime. Or perhaps Mark would want more conversation. "What do you think of girls?" he would ask again, and the discussion would follow its same course.

Charles grew old. His limbs lost their flexibility, and some of his wiring started to corrode. Mark would spend hours keeping the robot in repair.

"You're getting rusty," he would cackle.

"You're not so young yourself," Charles would reply. He had an answer for almost everything. Nothing involved, but an answer.

It was always night on Martha, but Mark broke up his time into mornings, afternoons and evenings. Their life followed a simple routine. Breakfast, from vegetables and Mark's canned store. Then the robot would work in the fields, and the plants grew used to his touch. Mark would repair the pump, check the water supply, and straighten up the immaculate shack. Lunch, and the robot's chores were usually finished.

The two would sit on the packing case and watch the stars. They would talk until supper, and sometimes late into the endless night.

In time, Mark built more complicated conversations into Charles. He couldn't give the robot free choice, of course, but he managed a pretty close approximation of it. Slowly, Charles' personality emerged. But it was strikingly different from Mark's.

Where Mark was querulous, Charles was calm. Mark was sardonic, Charles was naive. Mark was a cynic, Charles was an idealist. Mark was often sad; Charles was forever content.

And in time, Mark forgot he had built the answers into Charles. He ac-

cepted the robot as a friend, of about his own age. A friend of long years' standing.

"The thing I don't understand," Mark would say, "is why a man like you wants to live here. I mean, it's all right for me. No one cares about me, and I never gave much of a damn about anyone. But why you?"

"Here I have a whole world," Charles would reply, "where on Earth I had to share with billions. I have the stars, bigger and brighter than on Earth. I have all space around me, close, like still waters. And I have you, Mark."

"Now, don't go getting sentimental on me—"

"I'm not. Friendship counts. Love was lost long ago, Mark. The love of a girl named Martha, whom neither of us ever met. And that's a pity. But friendship remains, and the eternal night."

"You're a bloody poet," Mark would say, half admiringly. "A poor poet."

Time passed unnoticed by the stars, and the air pump hissed and clanked and leaked. Mark was fixing it constantly, but the air of Martha became increasingly rare. Although Charles labored in the fields, the crops, deprived of sufficient air, died.

Mark was tired now, and barely able to crawl around, even without the grip of gravity. He stayed in his bunk most of the time. Charles fed him as best he could, moving on rusty, creaking limbs.

"What do you think of girls?"

"I never saw a good one yet."

"Well, that's not fair."

Mark was too tired to see the end coming, and Charles wasn't interested. But the end was on its way. The air pump threatened to give out momentarily. There hadn't been any food for days.

"But why you?" Gasping in the escaping air. Strangling.

"Here I have a whole world—"

"Don't get sentimental—"

"And the love of a girl named Martha."

From his bunk Mark saw the stars for the last time. Big, bigger than ever, endlessly floating in the still waters of space.

"The stars ..." Mark said.

"Yes?"

"The sun?"

"—shall shine as now."

"A bloody poet."

"A poor poet."

"And girls?"

"I dreamed of a girl named Martha once. Maybe if—"

"What do you think of girls? And stars? And Earth?" And it was bedtime, this time forever.

Charles stood beside the body of his friend. He felt for a pulse once, and allowed the withered hand to fall. He walked to a corner of the shack and turned off the tired air pump.

The tape that Mark had prepared had a few cracked inches left to run. "I hope he finds his Martha," the robot croaked, and then the tape broke.

His rusted limbs would not bend, and he stood frozen, staring back at the naked stars. Then he bowed his head.

"The Lord is my shepherd," Charles said. "I shall not want. He maketh me to lie down in green pastures; he leadeth me ..."

Cost of Living

Illustrated by EMSH

*If easy payment plans were
to be really efficient, patrons'
lifetimes had to be extended!*

Carrin decided that he could trace his present mood to Miller's suicide last week. But the knowledge didn't help him get rid of the vague, formless fear in the back of his mind. It was foolish. Miller's suicide didn't concern him.

But why had that fat, jovial man killed himself? Miller had had everything to live for—wife, kids, good job, and all the marvelous luxuries of the age. Why had he done it?

"Good morning, dear," Carrin's wife said as he sat down at the breakfast table.

"Morning, honey. Morning, Billy."

His son grunted something.

You just couldn't tell about people, Carrin decided, and dialed his breakfast. The meal was gracefully prepared and served by the new Avignon Electric Auto-cook.

His mood persisted, annoyingly enough since Carrin wanted to be in top form this morning. It was his day off, and the Avignon Electric finance man was coming. This was an important day.

He walked to the door with his son.

"Have a good day, Billy."

His son nodded, shifted his books and started to school without answering. Carrin wondered if something was bothering him, too. He hoped not. One worrier in the family was plenty.

"See you later, honey." He kissed his wife as she left to go shopping.

At any rate, he thought, watching her go down the walk, at least she's happy. He wondered how much she'd spend at the A. E. store.

Checking his watch, he found that he had half an hour before the A. E. finance man was due. The best way to get rid of a bad mood was to drown it, he told himself, and headed for the shower.

The shower room was a glittering plastic wonder, and the sheer luxury of it eased Carrin's mind. He threw his clothes into the A. E. automatic Kleen-presser, and adjusted the shower spray to a notch above "brisk." The five-degrees-above-skin-temperature water beat against his thin white body. Delightful! And then a relaxing rub-dry in the A. E. Auto-towel.

Wonderful, he thought, as the towel stretched and kneaded his stringy muscles. And it should be wonderful, he reminded himself. The A. E. Auto-towel with shaving attachments had cost three hundred and thirteen dollars, plus tax.

But worth every penny of it, he decided, as the A. E. shaver came out of a corner and whisked off his rudimentary stubble. After all, what good was life if you couldn't enjoy the luxuries?

His skin tingled when he switched off the Auto-towel. He should have been feeling wonderful, but he wasn't. Miller's suicide kept nagging at his mind, destroying the peace of his day off.

Was there anything else bothering him? Certainly there was nothing wrong with the house. His papers were in order for the finance man.

"Have I forgotten something?" he asked out loud.

"The Avignon Electric finance man will be here in fifteen minutes," his A. E. bathroom Wall-reminder whispered.

"I know that. Is there anything else?"

The Wall-reminder reeled off its memorized data—a vast amount of minutiae about watering the lawn, having the Jet-lash checked, buying lamb chops for Monday, and the like. Things he still hadn't found time for.

"All right, that's enough." He allowed the A. E. Auto-dresser to dress him, skillfully draping a new selection of fabrics over his bony frame. A whiff of fashionable masculine perfume finished him and he went into the living room, threading his way between the appliances that lined the walls.

A quick inspection of the dials on the wall assured him that the house was in order. The breakfast dishes had been sanitized and stacked, the house had been cleaned, dusted, polished, his wife's garments had been hung up, his son's model rocket ships had been put back in the closet.

Stop worrying, you hypochondriac, he told himself angrily.

The door announced, "Mr. Pathis from Avignon Finance is here."

Carrin started to tell the door to open, when he noticed the Automatic Bartender.

Good God, why hadn't he thought of it!

The Automatic Bartender was manufactured by Castile Motors. He had bought it in a weak moment. A. E. wouldn't think very highly of that, since they sold their own brand.

He wheeled the bartender into the kitchen, and told the door to open.

"A very good day to you, sir," Mr. Pathis said.

Pathis was a tall, imposing man, dressed in a conservative tweed drape. His eyes had the crinkled corners of a man who laughs frequently. He beamed broadly and shook Carrin's hand, looking around the crowded living room.

"A beautiful place you have here, sir. Beautiful! As a matter of fact, I don't think I'll be overstepping the company's code to inform you that yours is the nicest interior in this section."

Carrin felt a sudden glow of pride at that, thinking of the rows of identical houses, on this block and the next, and the one after that.

"Now, then, is everything functioning properly?" Mr. Pathis asked, setting his briefcase on a chair. "Everything in order?"

"Oh, yes," Carrin said enthusiastically. "Avignon Electric never goes out of whack."

"The phone all right? Changes records for the full seventeen hours?"

"It certainly does," Carrin said. He hadn't had a chance to try out the phone, but it was a beautiful piece of furniture.

"The Solido-projector all right? Enjoying the programs?"

"Absolutely perfect reception." He had watched a program just last month, and it had been startlingly lifelike.

"How about the kitchen? Auto-cook in order? Recipe-master still knocking 'em out?"

"Marvelous stuff. Simply marvelous."

Mr. Pathis went on to inquire about his refrigerator, his vacuum cleaner, his car, his helicopter, his subterranean swimming pool, and the hundreds of other items Carrin had bought from Avignon Electric.

"Everything is swell," Carrin said, a trifle untruthfully since he hadn't unpacked every item yet. "Just wonderful."

"I'm so glad," Mr. Pathis said, leaning back with a sigh of relief. "You have no idea how hard we try to satisfy our customers. If a product isn't right, back it comes, no questions asked. We believe in pleasing our customers."

"I certainly appreciate it, Mr. Pathis."

Carrin hoped the A. E. man wouldn't ask to see the kitchen. He visualized the Castile Motors Bartender in there, like a porcupine in a dog show.

"I'm proud to say that most of the people in this neighborhood buy from us," Mr. Pathis was saying. "We're a solid firm."

"Was Mr. Miller a customer of yours?" Carrin asked.

"That fellow who killed himself?" Pathis frowned briefly. "He was, as a matter of fact. That amazed me, sir, absolutely amazed me. Why, just last month the fellow bought a brand-new Jet-lash from me, capable of doing three hundred and fifty miles an hour on a straightaway. He was as happy as a kid over it, and then to go and do a thing like that! Of course, the Jet-lash brought up his debt a little."

"Of course."

"But what did that matter? He had every luxury in the world. And then he went and hung himself."

"Hung himself?"

"Yes," Pathis said, the frown coming back. "Every modern convenience in his house, and he hung himself with a piece of rope. Probably unbalanced for a long time."

The frown slid off his face, and the customary smile replaced it. "But enough of that! Let's talk about you."

The smile widened as Pathis opened his briefcase. "Now, then, your account. You owe us two hundred and three thousand dollars and twenty-nine cents, Mr. Carrin, as of your last purchase. Right?"

"Right," Carrin said, remembering the amount from his own papers. "Here's my installment."

He handed Pathis an envelope, which the man checked and put in his pocket.

"Fine. Now you know, Mr. Carrin, that you won't live long enough to pay us the full two hundred thousand, don't you?"

"No, I don't suppose I will," Carrin said soberly.

He was only thirty-nine, with a full hundred years of life before him, thanks to the marvels of medical science. But at a salary of three thousand a year, he still couldn't pay it all off and have enough to support a family on at the same time.

"Of course, we would not want to deprive you of necessities, which in any case is fully protected by the laws we helped formulate and pass. To say nothing of the terrific items that are coming out next year. Things you wouldn't want to miss, sir!"

Mr. Carrin nodded. Certainly he wanted new items.

"Well, suppose we make the customary arrangement. If you will just sign over your son's earnings for the first thirty years of his adult life, we can easily arrange credit for you."

Mr. Pathis whipped the papers out of his briefcase and spread them in front of Carrin.

"If you'll just sign here, sir."

"Well," Carrin said, "I'm not sure. I'd like to give the boy a start in life, not saddle him with—"

"But my dear sir," Pathis interposed, "this is for your son as well. He lives here, doesn't he? He has a right to enjoy the luxuries, the marvels of science."

"Sure," Carrin said. "Only—"

"Why, sir, today the average man is living like a king. A hundred years ago the richest man in the world couldn't buy what any ordinary citizen possesses at present. You mustn't look upon it as a debt. It's an investment."

"That's true," Carrin said dubiously.

He thought about his son and his rocket ship models, his star charts, his maps. Would it be right? he asked himself.

"What's wrong?" Pathis asked cheerfully.

"Well, I was just wondering," Carrin said. "Signing over my son's earnings—you don't think I'm getting in a little too deep, do you?"

"Too deep? My dear sir!" Pathis exploded into laughter. "Do you know Mellon down the block? Well, don't say I said it, but he's already mortgaged his grandchildren's salary for their full life-expectancy! And he doesn't have half the goods he's made up his mind to own! We'll work out something for him. Service to the customer is our job and we know it well."

Carrin wavered visibly.

"And after you're gone, sir, they'll all belong to your son."

That was true, Carrin thought. His son would have all the marvelous things that filled the house. And after all, it was only thirty years out of a life expectancy of a hundred and fifty.

He signed with a flourish.

"Excellent!" Pathis said. "And by the way, has your home got an A. E. Master-operator?"

It hadn't. Pathis explained that a Master-operator was new this year, a stupendous advance in scientific engineering. It was designed to take over all the functions of housecleaning and cooking, without its owner having to lift a finger.

"Instead of running around all day, pushing half a dozen different buttons, with the Master-operator all you have to do is push one! A remarkable achievement!"

Since it was only five hundred and thirty-five dollars, Carrin signed for one, having it added to his son's debt.

Right's right, he thought, walking Pathis to the door. This house will be Billy's someday. His and his wife's. They certainly will want everything up-to-date.

Just one button, he thought. That would be a time-saver!

After Pathis left, Carrin sat back in an adjustable chair and turned on the solido. After twisting the Ezi-dial, he discovered that there was nothing he wanted to see. He tilted back the chair and took a nap.

The something on his mind was still bothering him.

"Hello, darling!" He awoke to find his wife was home. She kissed him on the ear. "Look."

She had bought an A. E. Sexitizer-negligee. He was pleasantly surprised that that was all she had bought. Usually, Leela returned from shopping laden down.

"It's lovely," he said.

She bent over for a kiss, then giggled—a habit he knew she had picked up from the latest popular solido star. He wished she hadn't.

"Going to dial supper," she said, and went to the kitchen. Carrin smiled, thinking that soon she would be able to dial the meals without moving out of the living room. He settled back in his chair, and his son walked in.

"How's it going, Son?" he asked heartily.

"All right," Billy answered listlessly.

"What'sa matter, Son?" The boy stared at his feet, not answering. "Come on, tell Dad what's the trouble."

Billy sat down on a packing case and put his chin in his hands. He looked thoughtfully at his father.

"Dad, could I be a Master Repairman if I wanted to be?"

Mr. Carrin smiled at the question. Billy alternated between wanting to be a Master Repairman and a rocket pilot. The repairmen were the elite. It was their job to fix the automatic repair machines. The repair machines could fix just about anything, but you couldn't have a machine fix the machine that fixed the machine. That was where the Master Repairmen came in.

But it was a highly competitive field and only a very few of the best brains were able to get their degrees. And, although the boy was bright, he didn't seem to have an engineering bent.

"It's possible, Son. Anything is possible."

"But is it possible for me?"

"I don't know," Carrin answered, as honestly as he could.

"Well, I don't want to be a Master Repairman anyway," the boy said, seeing that the answer was no. "I want to be a space pilot."

"A space pilot, Billy?" Leela asked, coming in to the room. "But there aren't any."

"Yes, there are," Billy argued. "We were told in school that the government is going to send some men to Mars."

"They've been saying that for a hundred years," Carrin said, "and they still haven't gotten around to doing it."

"They will this time."

"Why would you want to go to Mars?" Leela asked, winking at Carrin. "There are no pretty girls on Mars."

"I'm not interested in girls. I just want to go to Mars."

"You wouldn't like it, honey," Leela said. "It's a nasty old place with no air."

"It's got some air. I'd like to go there," the boy insisted sullenly. "I don't like it here."

"What's that?" Carrin asked, sitting up straight. "Is there anything you haven't got? Anything you want?"

"No, sir. I've got everything I want." Whenever his son called him 'sir,' Carrin knew that something was wrong.

"Look, Son, when I was your age I wanted to go to Mars, too. I wanted to do romantic things. I even wanted to be a Master Repairman."

"Then why didn't you?"

"Well, I grew up. I realized that there were more important things. First I had to pay off the debt my father had left me, and then I met your mother—"

Leela giggled.

"—and I wanted a home of my own. It'll be the same with you. You'll pay off your debt and get married, the same as the rest of us."

Billy was silent for a while, then he brushed his dark hair—straight, like his father's—back from his forehead and wet his lips.

"How come I have debts, sir?"

Carrin explained carefully. About the things a family needed for civilized living, and the cost of those items. How they had to be paid. How it was customary for a son to take on a part of his parent's debt, when he came of age.

Billy's silence annoyed him. It was almost as if the boy were reproaching him. After he had slaved for years to give the ungrateful whelp every luxury!

"Son," he said harshly, "have you studied history in school? Good. Then you know how it was in the past. Wars. How would you like to get blown up in a war?"

The boy didn't answer.

"Or how would you like to break your back for eight hours a day, doing work a machine should handle? Or be hungry all the time? Or cold, with the rain beating down on you, and no place to sleep?"

He paused for a response, got none and went on. "You live in the most fortunate age mankind has ever known. You are surrounded by every wonder of art and science. The finest music, the greatest books and art, all at your fingertips. All you have to do is push a button." He shifted to a kindlier tone. "Well, what are you thinking?"

"I was just wondering how I could go to Mars," the boy said. "With the debt, I mean. I don't suppose I could get away from that."

"Of course not."

"Unless I stowed away on a rocket."

"But you wouldn't do that."

"No, of course not," the boy said, but his tone lacked conviction.

"You'll stay here and marry a very nice girl," Leela told him.

"Sure I will," Billy said. "Sure." He grinned suddenly. "I didn't mean any of that stuff about going to Mars. I really didn't."

"I'm glad of that," Leela answered.

"Just forget I mentioned it," Billy said, smiling stiffly. He stood up and raced upstairs.

"Probably gone to play with his rockets," Leela said. "He's such a little devil."

The Carrins ate a quiet supper, and then it was time for Mr. Carrin to go to work. He was on night shift this month. He kissed his wife good-by, climbed into his Jet-lash and roared to the factory. The automatic gates recognized him and opened. He parked and walked in.

Automatic lathes, automatic presses—everything was automatic. The factory was huge and bright, and the machines hummed softly to themselves, doing their job and doing it well.

Carrin walked to the end of the automatic washing machine assembly line, to relieve the man there.

"Everything all right?" he asked.

"Sure," the man said. "Haven't had a bad one all year. These new models here have built-in voices. They don't light up like the old ones."

Carrin sat down where the man had sat and waited for the first washing machine to come through. His job was the soul of simplicity. He just sat there and the machines went by him. He pressed a button on them and found out if they were all right. They always were. After passing him, the washing machines went to the packaging section.

The first one slid by on the long slide of rollers. He pressed the starting button on the side.

"Ready for the wash," the washing machine said.

Carrin pressed the release and let it go by.

That boy of his, Carrin thought. Would he grow up and face his responsibilities? Would he mature and take his place in society? Carrin doubted it. The boy was a born rebel. If anyone got to Mars, it would be his kid.

But the thought didn't especially disturb him.

"Ready for the wash." Another machine went by.

Carrin remembered something about Miller. The jovial man had always been talking about the planets, always kidding about going off somewhere and roughing it. He hadn't, though. He'd committed suicide.

"Ready for the wash."

Carrin had eight hours in front of him, and he loosened his belt to prepare for it. Eight hours of pushing buttons and listening to a machine announce its readiness.

"Ready for the wash."

He pressed the release.

"Ready for the wash."

Carrin's mind strayed from the job, which didn't need much attention in any case. He wished he had done what he had longed to do as a youngster.

It would have been great to be a rocket pilot, to push a button and go to Mars.

Diplomatic Immunity

Illustrated by ASHMAN

He said he wasn't immortal—but nothing could kill him. Still, if the Earth was to live as a free world, he had to die.

Come right in, gentlemen," the Ambassador waved them into the very special suite the State Department had given him. "Please be seated."

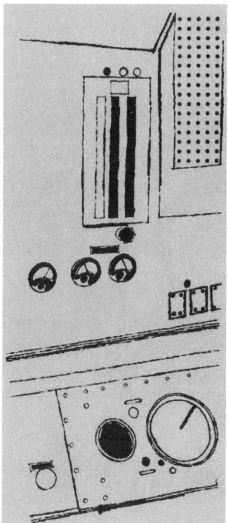

Colonel Cercy accepted a chair, trying to size up the individual who had all Washington chewing its fingernails. The Ambassador hardly looked like a menace. He was of medium height and slight build, dressed in a conservative brown tweed suit that the State Department had given him. His face was intelligent, finely molded and aloof.

As human as a human, Cercy thought, studying the alien with bleak, impersonal eyes.

"How may I serve you?" the Ambassador asked, smiling.

"The President has put me in charge of your case," Cercy said. "I've studied Professor Darrig's reports—" he nodded at the scientist beside him—"but I'd like to hear the whole thing for myself."

"Of course," the alien said, lighting a cigarette. He seemed genuinely pleased to be asked; which was interesting, Cercy thought. In the week since he had landed, every important scientist in the country had been at him.

But in a pinch they call the Army, Cercy reminded himself. He settled back in his chair, both hands jammed carelessly in his pockets. His right hand was resting on the butt of a .45, the safety off.

I have come," the alien said, "as an ambassador-at-large, representing an empire that stretches half-way across the Galaxy. I wish to extend the welcome of my people and to invite you to join our organization."

"I see," Cercy replied. "Some of the scientists got the impression that participation was compulsory."

"You will join," the Ambassador said, blowing smoke through his nostrils.

Cercy could see Darrig stiffen in his chair and bite his lip. Cercy moved the automatic to a position where he could draw it easily. "How did you find us?" he asked.

"We ambassadors-at-large are each assigned an unexplored section of space," the alien said. "We examine each star-system in that region for planets, and each planet for intelligent life. Intelligent life is rare in the Galaxy, you know."

Cercy nodded, although he hadn't been aware of the fact.

"When we find such a planet, we land, as I did, and prepare the inhabitants for their part in our organization."

"How will your people know that you have found intelligent life?" Cercy asked.

"There is a sending mechanism that is part of our structure," the Ambassador answered. "It is triggered when we reach an inhabited planet. This signal is beamed continually into space, to an effective range of several thousand light-years. Follow-up crews are continually sweeping through the limits of the reception area of each Ambassador, listening for such messages. Detecting

one, a colonizing team follows it to the planet."

He tapped his cigarette delicately on the edge of an ash tray. "This method has definite advantages over sending combined colonization and exploration teams obviously. It avoids the necessity of equipping large forces for what may be decades of searching."

"Sure." Cercy's face was expressionless. "Would you tell me more about this message?"

"There isn't much more you need know. The beam is not detectable by your methods and, therefore, cannot be jammed. The message continues as long as I am alive."

Darrig drew in his breath sharply, glancing at Cercy.

"If you stopped broadcasting," Cercy said casually, "our planet would never be found."

"Not until this section of space was resurveyed," the diplomat agreed.

"Very well. As a duly appointed representative of the President of the United States, I ask you to stop transmitting. We don't choose to become part of your empire."

"I'm sorry," the Ambassador said. He shrugged his shoulders easily. Cercy wondered how many times he had played this scene on how many other planets.

"There's really nothing I can do." He stood up.

"Then you won't stop?"

"I can't. I have no control over the sending, once it's activated." The diplomat turned and walked to the window. "However, I have prepared a philosophy for you. It is my duty, as your Ambassador, to ease the shock of transition as much as possible. This philosophy will make it instantly apparent that—"

As the Ambassador reached the window, Cercy's gun was out of his pocket and roaring. He squeezed six rounds in almost a single explosion, aiming at the Ambassador's head and back. Then an uncontrollable shudder ran through him.

The Ambassador was no longer there!

Cercy and Darrig stared at each other. Darrig muttered something about ghosts. Then, just as suddenly, the Ambassador was back.

"You didn't think," he said, "that it would be as easy as all that, did you? We Ambassadors have, necessarily, a certain diplomatic immunity." He fingered one of the bullet holes in the wall. "In case you don't understand, let me put it this way. It is not in your power to kill me. You couldn't even understand the nature of my defense."

He looked at them, and in that moment Cercy felt the Ambassador's complete alienness.

"Good day, gentlemen," he said.

Darrig and Cercy walked silently back to the control room. Neither had really expected that the Ambassador would be killed so easily, but it had still been a shock when the slugs had failed.

"I suppose you saw it all, Malley?" Cercy asked, when he reached the control room.

The thin, balding psychiatrist nodded sadly. "Got it on film, too."

"I wonder what his philosophy is," Darrig mused, half to himself.

"It was illogical to expect it would work. No race would send an ambassador with a message like that and expect him to live through it. Unless—"

"Unless what?"

"Unless he had a pretty effective defense," the psychiatrist finished unhappily.

Cercy walked across the room and looked at the video panel. The Ambassador's suite was very special. It had been hurriedly constructed two days after he had landed and delivered his message. The suite was steel and lead lined, filled with video and movie cameras, recorders, and a variety of other things.

It was the last word in elaborate death cells.

In the screen, Cercy could see the Ambassador sitting at a table. He was typing on a little portable the Government had given him.

"Hey, Harrison!" Cercy called. "Might as well go ahead with Plan Two."

Harrison came out of a side room where he had been examining the circuits leading to the Ambassador's suite. Methodically he checked his pressure gauges, set the controls and looked at Cercy. "Now?" he asked.

"Now." Cercy watched the screen. The Ambassador was still typing.

Suddenly, as Harrison sent home the switch, the room was engulfed in flames. Fire blasted out of concealed holes in the walls, poured from the ceiling and floor.

In a moment, the room was like the inside of a blast furnace.

Cercy let it burn for two minutes, then motioned Harrison to cut the switch. They stared at the roasted room.

They were looking, hopefully, for a charred corpse.

But the Ambassador reappeared beside his desk, looking ruefully at the charred typewriter. He was completely unsinged.

"Could you get me another typewriter?" he asked, looking directly at one of the hidden projectors. "I'm setting down a philosophy for you ungrateful wretches."

He seated himself in the wreckage of an armchair. In a moment, he was apparently asleep.

———————————————

All right, everyone grab a seat," Cercy said. "Time for a council of war."

Malley straddled a chair backward. Harrison lighted a pipe as he sat down, slowly puffing it into life.

"Now, then," Cercy said. "The Government has dropped this squarely in our laps. We have to kill the Ambassador—obviously. I've been put in charge." Cercy grinned with regret. "Probably because no one higher up wants the responsibility of failure. And I've selected you three as my staff. We can have anything we want, any assistance or advice we need. All right. Any ideas?"

"How about Plan Three?" Harrison asked.

"We'll get to that," Cercy said. "But I don't believe it's going to work."

"I don't either," Darrig agreed. "We don't even know the nature of his defense."

"That's the first order of business. Malley, take all our data so far, and get someone to feed it into the Derichman Analyzer. You know the stuff we want. What properties has X, if X can do thus and thus?"

"Right," Malley said. He left, muttering something about the ascendancy of the physical sciences.

"Harrison," Cercy asked, "is Plan Three set up?"

"Sure."

"Give it a try."

While Harrison was making his last adjustments, Cercy watched Darrig. The plump little physicist was staring thoughtfully into space, muttering to himself. Cercy hoped he would come up with something. He was expecting great things of Darrig.

Knowing the impossibility of working with great numbers of people, Cercy had picked his staff with care. Quality was what he wanted.

With that in mind, he had chosen Harrison first. The stocky, sour-faced engineer had a reputation for being able to build anything, given half an idea of how it worked.

Cercy had selected Malley, the psychiatrist, because he wasn't sure that killing the Ambassador was going to be a purely physical problem.

Darrig was a mathematical physicist, but his restless, curious mind had come up with some interesting theories in other fields. He was the only one of the four who was really interested in the Ambassador as an intellectual problem.

"He's like Metal Old Man," Darrig said finally.

"What's that?"

"Haven't you ever heard the story of Metal Old Man? Well, he was a monster covered with black metal armor. He was met by Monster-Slayer, an Apache culture hero. Monster-Slayer, after many attempts, finally killed Metal Old Man."

"How did he do it?"

"Shot him in the armpit. He didn't have any armor there."

"Fine," Cercy grinned. "Ask our Ambassador to raise his arm."

"All set!" Harrison called.

"Fine. Go."

In the Ambassador's room, an invisible spray of gamma rays silently began to flood the room with deadly radiation.

But there was no Ambassador to receive them.

"That's enough," Cercy said, after a while. "That would kill a herd of elephants."

But the Ambassador stayed invisible for five hours, until some of the radioactivity had abated. Then he appeared again.

"I'm still waiting for that typewriter," he said.

Here's the Analyzer's report." Malley handed Cercy a sheaf of papers. "This is the final formulation, boiled down."

Cercy read it aloud: "The simplest defense against any and all weapons, is to become each particular weapon."

"Great," Harrison said. "What does it mean?"

"It means," Darrig explained, "that when we attack the Ambassador with fire, he turns into fire. Shoot at him, and he turns into a bullet—until the menace is gone, and then he changes back again." He took the papers out of Cercy's hand and riffled through them.

"Hmm. Wonder if there's any historical parallel? Don't suppose so." He raised his head. "Although this isn't conclusive, it seems logical enough. Any other defense would involve recognition of the weapon first, then an appraisal, then a countermove predicated on the potentialities of the weapon. The Ambassador's defense would be a lot faster and safer. He wouldn't have to recognize the weapon. I suppose his body simply identifies, in some way, with the menace at hand."

"Did the Analyzer say there was any way of breaking this defense?" Cercy asked.

"The Analyzer stated definitely that there was no way, if the premise were true," Malley answered gloomily.

"We can discard that judgment," Darrig said. "The machine is limited."

"But we still haven't got any way of stopping him," Malley pointed out. "And he's still broadcasting that beam."

Cercy thought for a moment. "Call in every expert you can find. We're going to throw the book at the Ambassador. I know," he said, looking at Darrig's dubious expression, "but we have to try."

During the next few days, every combination and permutation of death was thrown at the Ambassador. He was showered with weapons, ranging from Stone-Age axes to modern high-powered rifles, peppered with hand grenades, drowned in acid, suffocated in poison gas.

He kept shrugging his shoulders philosophically, and continued to work on the new typewriter they had given him.

Bacteria was piped in, first the known germ diseases, then mutated species.

The diplomat didn't even sneeze.

He was showered with electricity, radiation, wooden weapons, iron weapons, copper weapons, brass weapons, uranium weapons—anything and everything, just to cover all possibilities.

He didn't suffer a scratch, but his room looked as though a bar-room brawl had been going on in it continually for fifty years.

Malley was working on an idea of his own, as was Darrig. The physicist interrupted himself long enough to remind Cercy of the Baldur myth. Baldur had been showered with every kind of weapon and remained unscathed, because everything on Earth had promised to love him. Everything, except the mistletoe. When a little twig of it was shot at him, he died.

Cercy turned away impatiently, but had an order of mistletoe sent up, just in case.

It was, at least, no less effective than the explosive shells or the bow and arrow. It did nothing except lend an oddly festive air to the battered room.

After a week of this, they moved the unprotesting Ambassador into a newer, bigger, stronger death cell. They were unable to venture into his old one because of the radioactivity and micro-organisms.

The Ambassador went back to work at his typewriter. All his previous attempts had been burned, torn or eaten away.

"Let's go talk to him," Darrig suggested, after another day had passed. Cercy agreed. For the moment, they were out of ideas.

Come right in, gentlemen," the Ambassador said, so cheerfully that Cercy felt sick. "I'm sorry I can't offer you anything. Through an oversight, I haven't been given any food or water for about ten days. Not that it matters, of course."

"Glad to hear it," Cercy said. The Ambassador hardly looked as if he had been facing all the violence Earth had to offer. On the contrary, Cercy and his men looked as though they had been under bombardment.

"You've got quite a defense there," Malley said conversationally.

"Glad you like it."

"Would you mind telling us how it works?" Darrig asked innocently.

"Don't you know?"

"We think so. You become what is attacking you. Is that right?"

"Certainly," the Ambassador said. "You see, I have no secrets from you."

"Is there anything we can give you," Cercy asked, "to get you to turn off that signal?"

"A bribe?"

"Sure," Cercy said. "Anything you—?"

"Nothing," the Ambassador replied.

"Look, be reasonable," Harrison said. "You don't want to cause a war, do you? Earth is united now. We're arming—"

"With what?"

"Atom bombs," Malley answered him. "Hydrogen bombs. We're—"

"Drop one on me," the Ambassador said. "It wouldn't kill me. What makes you think it will have any effect on my people?"

The four men were silent. Somehow, they hadn't thought of that.

"A people's ability to make war," the Ambassador stated, "is a measure of the status of their civilization. Stage one is the use of simple physical extensions. Stage two is control at the molecular level. You are on the threshold of stage three, although still far from mastery of atomic and subatomic forces." He smiled ingratiatingly. "My people are reaching the limits of stage five."

"What would that be?" Darrig asked.

"You'll find out," the Ambassador said. "But perhaps you've wondered if my powers are typical? I don't mind telling you that they're not. In order for me to do my job and nothing more, I have certain built-in restrictions, making me capable only of passive action."

"Why?" Darrig asked.

"For obvious reasons. If I were to take positive action in a moment of anger, I might destroy your entire planet."

"Do you expect us to believe that?" Cercy asked.

"Why not? Is it so hard to understand? Can't you believe that there are forces you know nothing about? And there is another reason for my passiveness. Certainly by this time you've deduced it?"

"To break our spirit, I suppose," Cercy said.

"Exactly. My telling you won't make any difference, either. The pattern is always the same. An Ambassador lands and delivers his message to a high-spirited, wild young race like yours. There is frenzied resistance against him, spasmodic attempts to kill him. After all these fail, the people are usually quite crestfallen. When the colonization team arrives, their indoctrination goes along just that much faster." He paused, then said, "Most planets are more interested in the philosophy I have to offer. I assure you, it will make the transition far easier."

He held out a sheaf of typewritten pages. "Won't you at least look through it?"

Darrig accepted the papers and put them in his pocket. "When I get time."

"I suggest you give it a try," the Ambassador said. "You must be near the crisis point now. Why not give it up?"

"Not yet," Cercy replied tonelessly.

"Don't forget to read the philosophy," the Ambassador urged them.

The men hurried from the room.

Now look," Malley said, once they were back in the control room, "there are a few things we haven't tried. How about utilizing psychology?"

"Anything you like," Cercy agreed, "including black magic. What did you have in mind?"

"The way I see it," Malley answered, "the Ambassador is geared to respond, instantaneously, to any threat. He must have an all-or-nothing defensive reflex. I suggest first that we try something that won't trigger that reflex."

"Like what?" Cercy asked.

"Hypnotism. Perhaps we can find out something."

"Sure," Cercy said. "Try it. Try anything."

Cercy, Malley and Darrig gathered around the video screen as an infinitesimal amount of a light hypnotic gas was admitted into the Ambassador's room. At the same time, a bolt of electricity lashed into the chair where the Ambassador was sitting.

"That was to distract him," Malley explained. The Ambassador vanished before the electricity struck him, and then appeared again, curled up in his armchair.

"That's enough," Malley whispered, and shut the valve. They watched. After a while, the Ambassador put down his book and stared into the distance.

"How strange," he said. "Alfern dead. Good friend ... just a freak accident. He ran into it, out there. Didn't have a chance. But it doesn't happen often."

"He's thinking out loud," Malley whispered, although there was no possibility of the Ambassador's hearing them. "Vocalizing his thoughts. His friend must have been on his mind for some time."

"Of course," the Ambassador went on, "Alfern had to die sometime. No immortality—yet. But that way—no defense. Out there in space they just pop up. Always there, underneath, just waiting for a chance to boil out."

"His body isn't reacting to the hypnotic as a menace yet," Cercy whispered.

"Well," the Ambassador told himself, "the regularizing principle has been doing pretty well, keeping it all down, smoothing out the inconsistencies—"

Suddenly he leaped to his feet, his face pale for a moment, as he obviously tried to remember what he had said. Then he laughed.

"Clever. That's the first time that particular trick has been played on me, and the last time. But, gentlemen, it didn't do you any good. I don't know, myself, how to go about killing me." He laughed at the blank walls.

"Besides," he continued, "the colonizing team must have the direction now. They'll find you with or without me."

He sat down again, smiling.

That does it!" Darrig cried. "He's not invulnerable. Something killed his friend Alfern."

"Something out in space," Cercy reminded him. "I wonder what it was."

"Let me see," Darrig reflected aloud. "The regularizing principle. That must be a natural law we knew nothing about. And underneath—what would be underneath?"

"He said the colonization team would find us anyhow," Malley reminded them.

"First things first," Cercy said. "He might have been bluffing us ... no,

I don't suppose so. We still have to get the Ambassador out of the way."

"I think I know what is underneath!" Darrig exclaimed. "This is wonderful. A new cosmology, perhaps."

"What is it?" Cercy asked. "Anything we can use?"

"I think so. But let me work it out. I think I'll go back to my hotel. I have some books there I want to check, and I don't want to be disturbed for a few hours."

"All right," Cercy agreed. "But what—?"

"No, no, I could be wrong," Darrig said. "Let me work it out." He hur-

ried from the room.

"What do you think he's driving at?" Malley asked.

"Beats me," Cercy shrugged. "Come on, let's try some more of that psychological stuff."

First they filled the Ambassador's room with several feet of water. Not enough to drown him, just enough to make him good and uncomfortable.

To this, they added the lights. For eight hours, lights flashed in the Ambassador's room. Bright lights to pry under his eyelids; dull, clashing ones to disturb him.

Sound came next—screeches and screams and shrill, grating noises. The sound of a man's fingernails being dragged across slate, amplified a thousand times, and strange, sucking noises, and shouts and whispers.

Then, the smells. Then, everything else they could think of that could drive a man insane.

The Ambassador slept peacefully through it all.

Now look," Cercy said, the following day, "let's start using our damned heads." His voice was hoarse and rough. Although the psychological torture hadn't bothered the Ambassador, it seemed to have backfired on Cercy and his men.

"Where in hell is Darrig?"

"Still working on that idea of his," Malley said, rubbing his stubbled chin. "Says he's just about got it."

"We'll work on the assumption that he can't produce," Cercy said. "Start thinking. For example, if the Ambassador can turn into anything, what is there he can't turn into?"

"Good question," Harrison grunted.

"It's the payoff question," Cercy said. "No use throwing a spear at a man who can turn into one."

"How about this?" Malley asked. "Taking it for granted he can turn into anything, how about putting him in a situation where he'll be attacked even after he alters?"

"I'm listening," Cercy said.

"Say he's in danger. He turns into the thing threatening him. What if that thing were itself being threatened? And, in turn, was in the act of threatening something else? What would he do then?"

"How are you going to put that into action?" Cercy asked.

"Like this." Malley picked up the telephone. "Hello? Give me the Washington Zoo. This is urgent."

The Ambassador turned as the door opened. An unwilling, angry, hungry tiger was propelled in. The door slammed shut.

The tiger looked at the Ambassador. The Ambassador looked at the tiger.

"Most ingenious," the Ambassador said.

At the sound of his voice, the tiger came unglued. He sprang like a steel spring uncoiling, landing on the floor where the Ambassador had been.

The door opened again. Another tiger was pushed in. He snarled angrily and leaped at the first. They smashed together in midair.

The Ambassador appeared a few feet off, watching. He moved back when a lion entered the door, head up and alert. The lion sprang at him, almost going over on his head when he struck nothing. Not finding any human, the lion leaped on one of the tigers.

The Ambassador reappeared in his chair, where he sat smoking and watching the beasts kill each other.

In ten minutes the room looked like an abattoir.

But by then the Ambassador had tired of the spectacle, and was reclining on his bed, reading.

I give up," Malley said. "That was my last bright idea."

Cercy stared at the floor, not answering. Harrison was seated in the corner, getting quietly drunk.

The telephone rang.

"Yeah?" Cercy said.

"I've got it!" Darrig's voice shouted over the line. "I really think this is it. Look, I'm taking a cab right down. Tell Harrison to find some helpers."

"What is it?" Cercy asked.

"The chaos underneath!" Darrig replied, and hung up.

They paced the floor, waiting for him to show up. Half an hour passed, then an hour. Finally, three hours after he had called, Darrig strolled in.

"Hello," he said casually.

"Hello, hell!" Cercy growled. "What kept you?"

"On the way over," Darrig said, "I read the Ambassador's philosophy. It's quite a work."

"Is that what took you so long?"

"Yes. I had the driver take me around the park a few times, while I was reading it."

"Skip it. How about—"

"I can't skip it," Darrig said, in a strange, tight voice. "I'm afraid we were wrong. About the aliens, I mean. It's perfectly right and proper that they should rule us. As a matter of fact, I wish they'd hurry up and get here."

But Darrig didn't look certain. His voice shook and perspiration poured from his face. He twisted his hands together, as though in agony.

"It's hard to explain," he said. "Everything became clear as soon as I started reading it. I saw how stupid we were, trying to be independent in this interdependent Universe. I saw—oh, look, Cercy. Let's stop all this foolishness and accept the Ambassador as our friend."

"Calm down!" Cercy shouted at the perfectly calm physicist. "You don't know what you're saying."

"It's strange," Darrig said. "I know how I felt—I just don't feel that way anymore. I think. Anyhow, I know your trouble. You haven't read the philosophy. You'll see what I mean, once you've read it." He handed Cercy the pile of papers. Cercy promptly ignited them with his cigarette lighter.

"It doesn't matter," Darrig said. "I've got it memorized. Just listen. Axiom one. All peoples—"

Cercy hit him, a short, clean blow, and Darrig slumped to the floor.

"Those words must be semantically keyed," Malley said. "They're designed to set off certain reactions in us, I suppose. All the Ambassador does is alter the philosophy to suit the peoples he's dealing with."

"Look, Malley," Cercy said. "This is your job now. Darrig knows, or thought he knew, the answer. You have to get that out of him."

"That won't be easy," Malley said. "He'd feel that he was betraying everything he believes in, if he were to tell us."

"I don't care how you get it," Cercy said. "Just get it."

"Even if it kills him?" Malley asked.

"Even if it kills you."

"Help me get him to my lab," Malley said.

That night Cercy and Harrison kept watch on the Ambassador from the control room. Cercy found his thoughts were racing in circles.

What had killed Alfern in space? Could it be duplicated on Earth? What was the regularizing principle? What was the chaos underneath?

What in hell am I doing here? he asked himself. But he couldn't start that sort of thing.

"What do you figure the Ambassador is?" he asked Harrison. "Is he a man?"

"Looks like one," Harrison said drowsily.

"But he doesn't act like one. I wonder if this is his true shape?"

Harrison shook his head, and lighted his pipe.

"What is there of him?" Cercy asked. "He looks like a man, but he can change into anything else. You can't attack him; he adapts. He's like water, taking the shape of any vessel he's poured into."

"You can boil water," Harrison yawned.

"Sure. Water hasn't any shape, has it? Or has it? What's basic?"

With an effort, Harrison tried to focus on Cercy's words. "Molecular pattern? The matrix?"

"Matrix," Cercy repeated, yawning himself. "Pattern. Must be something like that. A pattern is abstract, isn't it?"

"Sure. A pattern can be impressed on anything. What did I say?"

"Let's see," Cercy said. "Pattern. Matrix. Everything about the Ambassador is capable of change. There must be some unifying force that retains his personality. Something that doesn't change, no matter what contortions he goes through."

"Like a piece of string," Harrison murmured with his eyes closed.

"Sure. Tie it in knots, weave a rope out of it, wind it around your finger; it's still string."

"Yeah."

"But how do you attack a pattern?" Cercy asked. And why couldn't he get some sleep? To hell with the Ambassador and his hordes of colonists, he was going to close his eyes for a moment....

Wake up, Colonel!"

Cercy pried his eyes open and looked up at Malley. Besides him, Harrison was snoring deeply. "Did you get anything?"

"Not a thing," Malley confessed. "The philosophy must've had quite an effect on him. But it didn't work all the way. Darrig knew that he had wanted to kill the Ambassador, and for good and sufficient reasons. Although he felt differently now, he still had the feeling that he was betraying us. On the one hand, he couldn't hurt the Ambassador; on the other, he wouldn't hurt us."

"Won't he tell anything?"

"I'm afraid it's not that simple," Malley said. "You know, if you have an insurmountable obstacle that must be surmounted ... and also, I think the philosophy had an injurious effect on his mind."

"What are you trying to say?" Cercy got to his feet.

"I'm sorry," Malley apologized, "there wasn't a damned thing I could do. Darrig fought the whole thing out in his mind, and when he couldn't fight any longer, he—retreated. I'm afraid he's hopelessly insane."

"Let's see him."

They walked down the corridor to Malley's laboratory. Darrig was relaxed on a couch, his eyes glazed and staring.

"Is there any way of curing him?" Cercy asked.

"Shock therapy, maybe." Malley was dubious. "It'll take a long time. And he'll probably block out everything that had to do with producing this."

Cercy turned away, feeling sick. Even if Darrig could be cured, it would be too late. The aliens must have picked up the Ambassador's message by now and were undoubtedly heading for Earth.

"What's this?" Cercy asked, picking up a piece of paper that lay by Darrig's hand.

"Oh, he was doodling," Malley said. "Is there anything written on it?"

Cercy read aloud: "'Upon further consideration I can see that Chaos and the Gorgon Medusa are closely related.'"

"What does that mean?" Malley asked.

"I don't know," Cercy puzzled. "He was always interested in folklore."

"Sounds schizophrenic," the psychiatrist said.

Cercy read it again. "'Upon further consideration, I can see that Chaos and the Gorgon Medusa are closely related.'" He stared at it. "Isn't it possible," he asked Malley, "that he was trying to give us a clue? Trying to trick himself into giving and not giving at the same time?"

"It's possible," Malley agreed. "An unsuccessful compromise—But what could it mean?"

"Chaos." Cercy remembered Darrig's mentioning that word in his telephone call. "That was the original state of the Universe in Greek myth, wasn't it? The formlessness out of which everything came?"

"Something like that," Malley said. "And Medusa was one of those three sisters with the horrible faces."

Cercy stood for a moment, staring at the paper. Chaos ... Medusa ... and the organizing principle! Of course!

"I think—" He turned and ran from the room. Malley looked at him; then loaded a hypodermic and followed.

In the control room, Cercy shouted Harrison into consciousness.

"Listen," he said, "I want you to build something, quick. Do you hear me?"

"Sure." Harrison blinked and sat up. "What's the rush?"

"I know what Darrig wanted to tell us," Cercy said. "Come on, I'll tell you what I want. And Malley, put down that hypodermic. I haven't cracked. I want you to get me a book on Greek mythology. And hurry it up."

Finding a Greek mythology isn't an easy task at two o'clock in the morning. With the aid of FBI men, Malley routed a book dealer out of bed. He got his book and hurried back.

Cercy was red-eyed and excited, and Harrison and his helpers were working away at three crazy looking rigs. Cercy snatched the book from Malley, looked up one item, and put it down.

"Great work," he said. "We're all set now. Finished, Harrison?"

"Just about." Harrison and ten helpers were screwing in the last parts. "Will you tell me what this is?"

"Me too," Malley put in.

"I don't mean to be secretive," Cercy said. "I'm just in a hurry. I'll explain as we go along." He stood up. "Okay, let's wake up the Ambassador."

They watched the screen as a bolt of electricity leaped from the ceiling to the Ambassador's bed. Immediately, the Ambassador vanished.

"Now he's a part of that stream of electrons, right?" Cercy asked.

"That's what he told us," Malley said.

"But still keeping his pattern, within the stream," Cercy continued. "He has to, in order to get back into his own shape. Now we start the first disrupter."

Harrison hooked the machine into circuit, and sent his helpers away.

"Here's a running graph of the electron stream," Cercy said. "See the difference?" On the graph there was an irregular series of peaks and valleys, constantly shifting and leveling. "Do you remember when you hypnotized the Ambassador? He talked about his friend who'd been killed in space."

"That's right," Malley nodded. "His friend had been killed by something that had just popped up."

"He said something else," Cercy went on. "He told us that the basic organizing force of the Universe usually stopped things like that. What does that mean to you?"

"The organizing force," Malley repeated slowly. "Didn't Darrig say that that was a new natural law?"

"He did. But think of the implications, as Darrig did. If an organizing principle is engaged in some work, there must be something that opposes it. That which opposes organization is—"

"Chaos!"

"That's what Darrig thought, and what we should have seen. The chaos is underlying, and out of it there arose an organizing principle. This principle, if I've got it right, sought to suppress the fundamental chaos, to make all things regular.

"But the chaos still boils out in spots, as Alfern found out. Perhaps the organizational pattern is weaker in space. Anyhow, those spots are dangerous, until the organizing principle gets to work on them."

He turned to the panel. "Okay, Harrison. Throw in the second disrupter." The peaks and valleys altered on the graph. They started to mount in crazy, meaningless configurations.

"Take Darrig's message in the light of that. Chaos, we know, is underlying. Everything was formed out of it. The Gorgon Medusa was something that couldn't be looked upon. She turned men into stone, you recall, destroyed them. So, Darrig found a relationship between chaos and that which can't be looked upon. All with regard to the Ambassador, of course."

"The Ambassador can't look upon chaos!" Malley cried.

"That's it. The Ambassador is capable of an infinite number of alterations and permutations. But something—the matrix—can't change, because then there would be nothing left. To destroy something as abstract as a pattern, we need a state in which no pattern is possible. A state of chaos."

The third disrupter was thrown into circuit. The graph looked as if a drunken caterpillar had been sketching on it.

"Those disrupters are Harrison's idea," Cercy said. "I told him I wanted an electrical current with absolutely no coherent pattern. The disrupters are an extension of radio jamming. The first alters the electrical pattern. That's its purpose: to produce a state of patternlessness. The second tries to destroy the pattern left by the first; the third tries to destroy the pattern made by the first two. They're fed back then, and any remaining pattern is systematically destroyed in circuit ... I hope."

"This is supposed to produce a state of chaos?" Malley asked, looking into the screen.

For a while there was only the whining of the machines and the crazy doodling of the graph. Then, in the middle of the Ambassador's room, a spot appeared. It wavered, shrunk, expanded—

What happened was indescribable. All they knew was that everything within the spot had disappeared.

"Switch it off" Cercy shouted. Harrison cut the switch.

The spot continued to grow.

"How is it we're able to look at it?" Malley asked, staring at the screen.

"The shield of Perseus, remember?" Cercy said. "Using it as a mirror, he could look at Medusa."

"It's still growing!" Malley shouted.

"There was a calculated risk in all this," Cercy said. "There's always the possibility that the chaos may go on, unchecked. If that happens, it won't matter much what—"

The spot stopped growing. Its edges wavered and rippled, and then it started to shrink.

"The organizing principle," Cercy said, and collapsed into a chair.

"Any sign of the Ambassador?" he asked, in a few minutes.

The spot was still wavering. Then it was gone. Instantly there was an explosion. The steel walls buckled inward, but held. The screen went dead.

"The spot removed all the air from the room," Cercy explained, "as well as the furniture and the Ambassador."

"He couldn't take it," Malley said. "No pattern can cohere, in a state of patternlessness. He's gone to join Alfern."

Malley started to giggle. Cercy felt like joining him, but pulled himself together.

"Take it easy," he said. "We're not through yet."

"Sure we are! The Ambassador—"

"Is out of the way. But there's still an alien fleet homing in on this region of space. A fleet so strong we couldn't scratch it with an H-bomb. They'll be looking for us."

He stood up.

"Go home and get some sleep. Something tells me that tomorrow we're going to have to start figuring out some way of camouflaging a planet."

It's well established now that the way you put a question often deter-
mines not only the answer you'll get, but the type of answer possible. So ...
a mechanical answerer, geared to produce the ultimate revelations in ref-
erence to anything you want to know, might have unsuspected limitations.

Ask A Foolish Question

ANSWERER was built to last as long as was necessary—which was quite long, as some races judge time, and not long at all, according to others. But to Answerer, it was just long enough.

As to size, Answerer was large to some and small to others. He could be viewed as complex, although some believed that he was really very simple.

Answerer knew that he was as he should be. Above and beyond all else, he was The Answerer. He Knew.

Of the race that built him, the less said the better. They also Knew, and never said whether they found the knowledge pleasant.

They built Answerer as a service to less-sophisticated races, and departed in a unique manner. Where they went only Answerer knows.

Because Answerer knows everything.

Upon his planet, circling his sun, Answerer sat. Duration continued, long, as some judge duration, short as others judge it. But as it should be, to Answerer.

Within him were the Answers. He knew the nature of things, and why

things are as they are, and what they are, and what it all means.

Answerer could answer anything, provided it was a legitimate question. And he wanted to! He was eager to!

How else should an Answerer be?

What else should an Answerer do?

So he waited for creatures to come and ask.

"How do you feel, sir?" Morran asked, floating gently over to the old man.

"Better," Lingman said, trying to smile. No-weight was a vast relief. Even though Morran had expended an enormous amount of fuel, getting into space under minimum acceleration, Lingman's feeble heart hadn't liked it. Lingman's heart had balked and sulked, pounded angrily against the brittle rib-case, hesitated and sped up. It seemed for a time as though Lingman's heart was going to stop, out of sheer pique.

But no-weight was a vast relief, and the feeble heart was going again.

Morran had no such problems. His strong body was built for strain and stress. He wouldn't experience them on this trip, not if he expected old Lingman to live.

"I'm going to live," Lingman muttered, in answer to the unspoken question. "Long enough to find out." Morran touched the controls, and the ship slipped into sub-space like an eel into oil.

"We'll find out," Morran murmured. He helped the old man unstrap himself. "We're going to find the Answerer!"

Lingman nodded at his young partner. They had been reassuring themselves for years. Originally it had been Lingman's project. Then Morran, graduating from Cal Tech, had joined him. Together they had traced the rumors across the solar system. The legends of an ancient humanoid race who had known the answer to all things, and who had built Answerer and departed.

"Think of it," Morran said. "The answer to everything!" A physicist, Morran had many questions to ask Answerer. The expanding universe; the binding force of atomic nuclei; novae and supernovae; planetary formation; red shift, relativity and a thousand others.

"Yes," Lingman said. He pulled himself to the vision plate and looked out on the bleak prairie of the illusory sub-space. He was a biologist and an old man. He had two questions.

What is life?

What is death?

AFTER a particularly-long period of hunting purple, Lek and his friends gathered to talk. Purple always ran thin in the neighborhood of multiple-cluster stars—why, no one knew—so talk was definitely in order.

"Do you know," Lek said, "I think I'll hunt up this Answerer." Lek spoke the Ollgrat language now, the language of imminent decision.

"Why?" Ilm asked him, in the Hvest tongue of light banter. "Why do you want to know things? Isn't the job of gathering purple enough for you?"

"No," Lek said, still speaking the language of imminent decision. "It is not." The great job of Lek and his kind was the gathering of purple. They found purple imbedded in many parts of the fabric of space, minute quantities of it. Slowly, they were building a huge mound of it. What the mound was for, no one knew.

"I suppose you'll ask him what purple is?" Ilm asked, pushing a star out of his way and lying down.

"I will," Lek said. "We have continued in ignorance too long. We must know the true nature of purple, and its meaning in the scheme of things. We must know why it governs our lives." For this speech Lek switched to Ilgret, the language of incipient-knowledge.

Ilm and the others didn't try to argue, even in the tongue of arguments. They knew that the knowledge was important. Ever since the dawn of time, Lek, Ilm and the others had gathered purple. Now it was time to know the ultimate answers to the universe—what purple was, and what the mound was for.

And of course, there was the Answerer to tell them. Everyone had heard of the Answerer, built by a race not unlike themselves, now long departed.

"Will you ask him anything else?" Ilm asked Lek.

"I don't know," Lek said. "Perhaps I'll ask about the stars. There's really nothing else important." Since Lek and his brothers had lived since the dawn of time, they didn't consider death. And since their numbers were always the same, they didn't consider the question of life.

But purple? And the mound?

"I go!" Lek shouted, in the vernacular of decision-to-fact.

"Good fortune!" his brothers shouted back, in the jargon of greatest-friendship.

Lek strode off, leaping from star to star.

Alone on his little planet, Answerer sat, waiting for the Questioners. Occasionally he mumbled the answers to himself. This was his privilege. He Knew.

But he waited, and the time was neither too long nor too short, for any of the creatures of space to come and ask.

THERE were eighteen of them, gathered in one place.

"I invoke the rule of eighteen," cried one. And another appeared, who had never before been, born by the rule of eighteen.

"We must go to the Answerer," one cried. "Our lives are governed by the rule of eighteen. Where there are eighteen, there will be nineteen. Why is this so?"

No one could answer.

"Where am I?" asked the newborn nineteenth. One took him aside for instruction.

That left seventeen. A stable number.

"And we must find out," cried another, "Why all places are different, although there is no distance."

That was the problem. One is here. Then one is there. Just like that, no movement, no reason. And yet, without moving, one is in another place.

"The stars are cold," one cried.

"Why?"

"We must go to the Answerer."

For they had heard the legends, knew the tales. "Once there was a race, a good deal like us, and they Knew—and they told Answerer. Then they departed to where there is no place, but much distance."

"How do we get there?" the newborn nineteenth cried, filled now with knowledge.

"We go." And eighteen of them vanished. One was left. Moodily he stared at the tremendous spread of an icy star, then he too vanished.

"Those old legends are true," Morran gasped. "There it is."

They had come out of sub-space at the place the legends told of, and before them was a star unlike any other star. Morran invented a classification for it, but it didn't matter. There was no other like it.

Swinging around the star was a planet, and this too was unlike any other planet. Morran invented reasons, but they didn't matter. This planet was the only one.

"Strap yourself in, sir," Morran said. "I'll land as gently as I can."

Lek came to Answerer, striding swiftly from star to star. He lifted Answerer in his hand and looked at him.

"So you are Answerer," he said.

"Yes," Answerer said.

"Then tell me," Lek said, settling himself comfortably in a gap between the stars, "Tell me what I am."

"A partiality," Answerer said. "An indication."

"Come now," Lek muttered, his pride hurt. "You can do better than that. Now then. The purpose of my kind is to gather purple, and to build a mound of it. Can you tell me the real meaning of this?"

"Your question is without meaning," Answerer said. He knew what purple actually was, and what the mound was for. But the explanation was concealed in a greater explanation. Without this, Lek's question was inexplicable, and Lek had failed to ask the real question.

Lek asked other questions, and Answerer was unable to answer them. Lek viewed things through his specialized eyes, extracted a part of the truth and refused to see more. How to tell a blind man the sensation of green?

Answerer didn't try. He wasn't supposed to.

Finally, Lek emitted a scornful laugh. One of his little stepping-stones flared at the sound, then faded back to its usual intensity.

Lek departed, striding swiftly across the stars.

Answerer knew. But he had to be asked the proper questions first. He pondered this limitation, gazing at the stars which were neither large nor small, but exactly the right size.

The proper questions. The race which built Answerer should have taken that into account, Answerer thought. They should have made some allowance for semantic nonsense, allowed him to attempt an unraveling.

Answerer contented himself with muttering the answers to himself.

EIGHTEEN creatures came to Answerer, neither walking nor flying, but simply appearing. Shivering in the cold glare of the stars, they gazed up at the massiveness of Answerer.

"If there is no distance," one asked, "Then how can things be in other places?"

Answerer knew what distance was, and what places were. But he couldn't answer the question. There was distance, but not as these creatures saw it. And there were places, but in a different fashion from that which the creatures expected.

"Rephrase the question," Answerer said hopefully.

"Why are we short here," one asked, "And long over there? Why are we fat over there, and short here? Why are the stars cold?"

Answerer knew all things. He knew why stars were cold, but he couldn't explain it in terms of stars or coldness.

"Why," another asked, "Is there a rule of eighteen? Why, when eighteen gather, is another produced?"

But of course the answer was part of another, greater question, which hadn't been asked.

Another was produced by the rule of eighteen, and the nineteen creatures vanished.

Answerer mumbled the right questions to himself, and answered them.

"We made it," Morran said. "Well, well." He patted Lingman on the shoulder—lightly, because Lingman might fall apart.

The old biologist was tired. His face was sunken, yellow, lined. Already the mark of the skull was showing in his prominent yellow teeth, his small, flat nose, his exposed cheekbones. The matrix was showing through.

"Let's get on," Lingman said. He didn't want to waste any time. He didn't have any time to waste.

Helmeted, they walked along the little path.

"Not so fast," Lingman murmured.

"Right," Morran said. They walked together, along the dark path of the planet that was different from all other planets, soaring alone around a sun different from all other suns.

"Up here," Morran said. The legends were explicit. A path, leading to stone steps. Stone steps to a courtyard. And then—the Answerer!

To them, Answerer looked like a white screen set in a wall. To their eyes, Answerer was very simple.

Lingman clasped his shaking hands together. This was the culmination of a lifetime's work, financing, arguing, ferreting bits of legend, ending here, now.

"Remember," he said to Morran, "We will be shocked. The truth will be like nothing we have imagined."

"I'm ready," Morran said, his eyes rapturous.

"Very well. Answerer," Lingman said, in his thin little voice, "What is life?"

A voice spoke in their heads. "The question has no meaning. By 'life,' the Questioner is referring to a partial phenomenon, inexplicable except in terms of its whole."

"Of what is life a part?" Lingman asked.

"This question, in its present form, admits of no answer. Questioner is still considering 'life,' from his personal, limited bias."

"Answer it in your own terms, then," Morran said.

"The Answerer can only answer questions." Answerer thought again of the sad limitation imposed by his builders.

Silence.

"Is the universe expanding?" Morran asked confidently.

"'Expansion' is a term inapplicable to the situation. Universe, as the Questioner views it, is an illusory concept."

"Can you tell us anything?" Morran asked.

"I can answer any valid question concerning the nature of things."

THE two men looked at each other.

"I think I know what he means," Lingman said sadly. "Our basic assumptions are wrong. All of them."

"They can't be," Morran said. "Physics, biology—"

"Partial truths," Lingman said, with a great weariness in his voice. "At least we've determined that much. We've found out that our inferences concerning observed phenomena are wrong."

"But the rule of the simplest hypothesis—"

"It's only a theory," Lingman said.

"But life—he certainly could answer what life is?"

"Look at it this way," Lingman said. "Suppose you were to ask, 'Why was I born under the constellation Scorpio, in conjunction with Saturn?' I would be unable to answer your question in terms of the zodiac, because the zodiac has nothing to do with it."

"I see," Morran said slowly. "He can't answer questions in terms of our assumptions."

"That seems to be the case. And he can't alter our assumptions. He is limited to valid questions—which imply, it would seem, a knowledge we just don't have."

"We can't even ask a valid question?" Morran asked. "I don't believe that. We must know some basics." He turned to Answerer. "What is death?"

"I cannot explain an anthropomorphism."

"Death an anthropomorphism!" Morran said, and Lingman turned quickly. "Now we're getting somewhere!"

"Are anthropomorphisms unreal?" he asked.

"Anthropomorphisms may be classified, tentatively, as, A, false truths, or B, partial truths in terms of a partial situation."

"Which is applicable here?"

"Both."

That was the closest they got. Morran was unable to draw any more from Answerer. For hours the two men tried, but truth was slipping farther and farther away.

"It's maddening," Morran said, after a while. "This thing has the answer to the whole universe, and he can't tell us unless we ask the right question. But how are we supposed to know the right question?"

Lingman sat down on the ground, leaning against a stone wall. He closed his eyes.

"Savages, that's what we are," Morran said, pacing up and down in front of Answerer. "Imagine a bushman walking up to a physicist and asking him why he can't shoot his arrow into the sun. The scientist can explain it only in his own terms. What would happen?"

"The scientist wouldn't even attempt it," Lingman said, in a dim voice; "he would know the limitations of the questioner."

"It's fine," Morran said angrily. "How do you explain the earth's rotation to a bushman? Or better, how do you explain relativity to him—maintaining scientific rigor in your explanation at all times, of course."

Lingman, eyes closed, didn't answer.

"We're bushmen. But the gap is much greater here. Worm and superman, perhaps. The worm desires to know the nature of dirt, and why there's so much of it. Oh, well."

"Shall we go, sir?" Morran asked. Lingman's eyes remained closed. His taloned fingers were clenched, his cheeks sunk further in. The skull was emerging.

"Sir! Sir!"

And Answerer knew that that was not the answer.

ALONE on his planet, which is neither large nor small, but exactly the right size, Answerer waits. He cannot help the people who come to him, for even Answerer has restrictions.

He can answer only valid questions.

Universe? Life? Death? Purple? Eighteen?

Partial truths, half-truths, little bits of the great question.

But Answerer, alone, mumbles the questions to himself, the true questions, which no one can understand.

How could they understand the true answers?

The questions will never be asked, and Answerer remembers something his builders knew and forgot.

In order to ask a question you must already know most of the answer.

The Leech

Illustrated by CONNELL

A visitor should be fed, but this one could eat you out of house and home ... literally!

The leech was waiting for food. For millennia it had been drifting across the vast emptiness of space. Without consciousness, it had spent the countless centuries in the void between the stars. It was unaware when it finally reached a sun. Life-giving radiation flared around the hard, dry spore. Gravitation tugged at it.

A planet claimed it, with other stellar debris, and the leech fell, still dead-seeming within its tough spore case.

One speck of dust among many, the winds blew it around the Earth, played with it, and let it fall.

On the ground, it began to stir. Nourishment soaked in, permeating the spore case. It grew—and fed.

Frank Conners came up on the porch and coughed twice. "Say, pardon me, Professor," he said.

The long, pale man didn't stir from the sagging couch. His horn-rimmed glasses were perched on his forehead, and he was snoring very gently.

"I'm awful sorry to disturb you," Conners said, pushing back his battered felt hat. "I know it's your restin' week and all, but there's something damned funny in the ditch."

The pale man's left eyebrow twitched, but he showed no other sign of having heard.

Frank Conners coughed again, holding his spade in one purple-veined hand. "Didja hear me, Professor?"

"Of course I heard you," Micheals said in a muffled voice, his eyes still closed. "You found a pixie."

"A what?" Conners asked, squinting at Micheals.

"A little man in a green suit. Feed him milk, Conners."

"No, sir. I think it's a rock."

Micheals opened one eye and focused it in Conners' general direction.

"I'm awfully sorry about it," Conners said. Professor Micheals' resting week was a ten-year-old custom, and his only eccentricity. All winter Micheals taught anthropology, worked on half a dozen committees, dabbled in physics and chemistry, and still found time to write a book a year. When summer came, he was tired.

Arriving at his worked-out New York State farm, it was his invariable rule to do absolutely nothing for a week. He hired Frank Conners to cook for that week and generally make himself useful, while Professor Micheals slept.

During the second week, Micheals would wander around, look at the trees and fish. By the third week he would be getting a tan, reading, repairing the sheds and climbing mountains. At the end of four weeks, he could hardly wait to get back to the city.

But the resting week was sacred.

"I really wouldn't bother you for anything small," Conners said apologetically. "But that damned rock melted two inches off my spade."

Micheals opened both eyes and sat up. Conners held out the spade. The rounded end was sheared cleanly off. Micheals swung himself off the couch and slipped his feet into battered moccasins.

"Let's see this wonder," he said.

The object was lying in the ditch at the end of the front lawn, three feet from the main road. It was round, about the size of a truck tire, and solid throughout. It was about an inch thick, as far as he could tell, grayish black and intricately veined.

"Don't touch it," Conners warned.

"I'm not going to. Let me have your spade." Micheals took the spade and prodded the object experimentally. It was completely unyielding. He held the spade to the surface for a moment, then withdrew it. Another inch was gone.

Micheals frowned, and pushed his glasses tighter against his nose. He held the spade against the rock with one hand, the other held close to the surface. More of the spade disappeared.

"Doesn't seem to be generating heat," he said to Conners. "Did you notice any the first time?"

Conners shook his head.

Micheals picked up a clod of dirt and tossed it on the object. The dirt dissolved quickly, leaving no trace on the gray-black surface. A large stone followed the dirt, and disappeared in the same way.

"Isn't that just about the damnedest thing you ever saw, Professor?" Conners asked.

"Yes," Micheals agreed, standing up again. "It just about is."

He hefted the spade and brought it down smartly on the object. When it hit, he almost dropped the spade. He had been gripping the handle rigidly, braced for a recoil. But the spade struck that unyielding surface and stayed. There was no perceptible give, but absolutely no recoil.

"Whatcha think it is?" Conners asked.

"It's no stone," Micheals said. He stepped back. "A leech drinks blood. This thing seems to be drinking dirt. And spades." He struck it a few more times, experimentally. The two men looked at each other. On the road, half a dozen Army trucks rolled past.

"I'm going to phone the college and ask a physics man about it," Micheals said. "Or a biologist. I'd like to get rid of that thing before it spoils my lawn."

They walked back to the house.

Everything fed the leech. The wind added its modicum of kinetic energy, ruffling across the gray-black surface. Rain fell, and the force of each individual drop added to its store. The water was sucked in by the all-absorbing surface.

The sunlight above it was absorbed, and converted into mass for its body. Beneath it, the soil was consumed, dirt, stones and branches broken down by the leech's complex cells and changed into energy. Energy was converted back into mass, and the leech grew.

Slowly, the first flickers of consciousness began to return. Its first realization was of the impossible smallness of its body.

It grew.

When Micheals looked the next day, the leech was eight feet across, sticking out into the road and up the side of the lawn. The following day it was almost eighteen feet in diameter, shaped to fit the contour of the ditch, and covering most of the road. That day the sheriff drove up in his model A, followed by half the town.

"Is that your leech thing, Professor Micheals?" Sheriff Flynn asked.

"That's it," Micheals said. He had spent the past days looking unsuccessfully for an acid that would dissolve the leech.

"We gotta get it out of the road," Flynn said, walking truculently up to the leech. "Something like this, you can't let it block the road, Professor. The Army's gotta use this road."

"I'm terribly sorry," Micheals said with a straight face. "Go right ahead, Sheriff. But be careful. It's hot." The leech wasn't hot, but it seemed the simplest explanation under the circumstances.

Micheals watched with interest as the sheriff tried to shove a crowbar under it. He smiled to himself when it was removed with half a foot of its length gone.

The sheriff wasn't so easily discouraged. He had come prepared for a stubborn piece of rock. He went to the rumble seat of his car and took out a blowtorch and a sledgehammer, ignited the torch and focused it on one edge of the leech.

After five minutes, there was no change. The gray didn't turn red or even seem to heat up. Sheriff Flynn continued to bake it for fifteen minutes, then called to one of the men.

"Hit that spot with the sledge, Jerry."

Jerry picked up the sledgehammer, motioned the sheriff back, and swung it over his head. He let out a howl as the hammer struck unyieldingly. There wasn't a fraction of recoil.

In the distance they heard the roar of an Army convoy.

"Now we'll get some action," Flynn said.

Micheals wasn't so sure. He walked around the periphery of the leech, asking himself what kind of substance would react that way. The answer was easy—no substance. No known substance.

The driver in the lead jeep held up his hand, and the long convoy ground to a halt. A hard, efficient-looking officer stepped out of the jeep. From the star on either shoulder, Micheals knew he was a brigadier general.

"You can't block this road," the general said. He was a tall, spare man in suntans, with a sunburned face and cold eyes. "Please clear that thing away."

"We can't move it," Micheals said. He told the general what had happened in the past few days.

"It must be moved," the general said. "This convoy must go through."

He walked closer and looked at the leech. "You say it can't be jacked up by a crowbar? A torch won't burn it?"

"That's right," Micheals said, smiling faintly.

"Driver," the general said over his shoulder. "Ride over it."

Micheals started to protest, but stopped himself. The military mind would have to find out in its own way.

The driver put his jeep in gear and shot forward, jumping the leech's four-inch edge. The jeep got to the center of the leech and stopped.

"I didn't tell you to stop!" the general bellowed.

"I didn't, sir!" the driver protested.

The jeep had been yanked to a stop and had stalled. The driver started it again, shifted to four-wheel drive, and tried to ram forward. The jeep was fixed immovably, as though set in concrete.

"Pardon me," Micheals said. "If you look, you can see that the tires are melting down."

The general stared, his hand creeping automatically toward his pistol belt. Then he shouted, "Jump, driver! Don't touch that gray stuff."

White-faced, the driver climbed to the hood of his jeep, looked around him, and jumped clear.

There was complete silence as everyone watched the jeep. First its tires melted down, and then the rims. The body, resting on the gray surface, melted, too.

The aerial was the last to go.

The general began to swear softly under his breath. He turned to the driver. "Go back and have some men bring up hand grenades and dynamite."

The driver ran back to the convoy.

"I don't know what you've got here," the general said. "But it's not going to stop a U.S. Army convoy."

Micheals wasn't so sure.

The leech was nearly awake now, and its body was calling for more and more food. It dissolved the soil under it at a furious rate, filling it in with its own body, flowing outward.

A large object landed on it, and that became food also. Then suddenly—

A burst of energy against its surface, and then another, and another. It consumed them gratefully, converting them into mass. Little metal pellets struck it, and their kinetic energy was absorbed, their mass converted. More explosions took place, helping to fill the starving cells.

It began to sense things—controlled combustion around it, vibrations of wind, mass movements.

There was another, greater explosion, a taste of real food! Greedily it ate, growing faster. It waited anxiously for more explosions, while its cells screamed for food.

But no more came. It continued to feed on the soil and on the Sun's energy. Night came, noticeable for its lesser energy possibilities, and then more days and nights. Vibrating objects continued to move around it.

It ate and grew and flowed.

Micheals stood on a little hill, watching the dissolution of his house. The leech was several hundred yards across now, lapping at his front porch.

Good-by, home, Micheals thought, remembering the ten summers he had spent there.

The porch collapsed into the body of the leech. Bit by bit, the house crumpled.

The leech looked like a field of lava now, a blasted spot on the green Earth.

"Pardon me, sir," a soldier said, coming up behind him. "General O'Donnell would like to see you."

"Right," Micheals said, and took his last look at the house.

He followed the soldier through the barbed wire that had been set up in a half-mile circle around the leech. A company of soldiers was on guard around it, keeping back the reporters and the hundreds of curious people who had flocked to the scene. Micheals wondered why he was still allowed inside. Probably, he decided, because most of this was taking place on his land.

The soldier brought him to a tent. Micheals stooped and went in. General O'Donnell, still in suntans, was seated at a small desk. He motioned Micheals to a chair.

"I've been put in charge of getting rid of this leech," he said to Micheals.

Micheals nodded, not commenting on the advisability of giving a soldier a scientist's job.

"You're a professor, aren't you?"

"Yes. Anthropology."

"Good. Smoke?" The general lighted Micheals' cigarette. "I'd like you to stay around here in an advisory capacity. You were one of the first to see this leech. I'd appreciate your observations on—" he smiled—"the enemy."

"I'd be glad to," Micheals said. "However, I think this is more in the line of a physicist or a biochemist."

"I don't want this place cluttered with scientists," General O'Donnell said, frowning at the tip of his cigarette. "Don't get me wrong. I have the greatest appreciation for science. I am, if I do say so, a scientific soldier. I'm always interested in the latest weapons. You can't fight any kind of a war any more without science."

O'Donnell's sunburned face grew firm. "But I can't have a team of long-hairs poking around this thing for the next month, holding me up. My job is to destroy it, by any means in my power, and at once. I am going to do just that."

"I don't think you'll find it that easy," Micheals said.

"That's what I want you for," O'Donnell said. "Tell me why and I'll figure out a way of doing it."

"Well, as far as I can figure out, the leech is an organic mass-energy converter, and a frighteningly efficient one. I would guess that it has a double cycle. First, it converts mass into energy, then back into mass for its body. Second, energy is converted directly into the body mass. How this takes place, I do not know. The leech is not protoplasmic. It may not even be cellular—"

"So we need something big against it," O'Donnell interrupted. "Well, that's all right. I've got some big stuff here."

"I don't think you understand me," Micheals said. "Perhaps I'm not phrasing this very well. The leech eats energy. It can consume the strength of any energy weapon you use against it."

"What happens," O'Donnell asked, "if it keeps on eating?"

"I have no idea what its growth-limits are," Micheals said. "Its growth may be limited only by its food source."

"You mean it could continue to grow probably forever?"

"It could possibly grow as long as it had something to feed on."

"This is really a challenge," O'Donnell said. "That leech can't be totally impervious to force."

"It seems to be. I suggest you get some physicists in here. Some biologists also. Have them figure out a way of nullifying it."

The general put out his cigarette. "Professor, I cannot wait while scientists wrangle. There is an axiom of mine which I am going to tell you." He paused impressively. "Nothing is impervious to force. Muster enough force and anything will give. Anything.

"Professor," the general continued, in a friendlier tone, "you shouldn't sell short the science you represent. We have, massed under North Hill, the greatest accumulation of energy and radioactive weapons ever assembled in one spot. Do you think your leech can stand the full force of them?"

"I suppose it's possible to overload the thing," Micheals said doubtfully. He realized now why the general wanted him around. He supplied the trappings of science, without the authority to override O'Donnell.

"Come with me," General O'Donnell said cheerfully, getting up and holding back a flap of the tent. "We're going to crack that leech in half."

After a long wait, rich food started to come again, piped into one side of it. First there was only a little, and then more and more. Radiations, vibrations, explosions, solids, liquids—an amazing variety of edibles. It accepted them all. But the food was coming too slowly for the starving cells, for new cells were constantly adding their demands to the rest.

The ever-hungry body screamed for more food, faster!

Now that it had reached a fairly efficient size, it was fully awake. It puzzled over the energy-impressions around it, locating the source of the new food massed in one spot.

Effortlessly it pushed itself into the air, flew a little way and dropped on the food. Its super-efficient cells eagerly gulped the rich radioactive substances. But it did not ignore the lesser potentials of metal and clumps of carbohydrates.

"The damned fools," General O'Donnell said. "Why did they have to panic? You'd think they'd never been trained." He paced the ground outside his tent, now in a new location three miles back.

The leech had grown to two miles in diameter. Three farming communities had been evacuated.

Micheals, standing beside the general, was still stupefied by the memory. The leech had accepted the massed power of the weapons for a while, and then its entire bulk had lifted in the air. The Sun had been blotted out as it flew leisurely over North Hill, and dropped. There should have been time for evacuation, but the frightened soldiers had been blind with fear.

Sixty-seven men were lost in Operation Leech, and General O'Donnell asked permission to use atomic bombs. Washington sent a group of scientists to investigate the situation.

"Haven't those experts decided yet?" O'Donnell asked, halting angrily in front of the tent. "They've been talking long enough."

"It's a hard decision," Micheals said. Since he wasn't an official member of the investigating team, he had given his information and left. "The physicists consider it a biological matter, and the biologists seem to think the chemists should have the answer. No one's an expert on this, because it's never happened before. We just don't have the data."

"It's a military problem," O'Donnell said harshly. "I'm not interested in what the thing is—I want to know what can destroy it. They'd better give me permission to use the bomb."

Micheals had made his own calculations on that. It was impossible to say for sure, but taking a flying guess at the leech's mass-energy absorption rate, figuring in its size and apparent capacity for growth, an atomic bomb might overload it—if used soon enough.

He estimated three days as the limit of usefulness. The leech was growing at a geometric rate. It could cover the United States in a few months.

"For a week I've been asking permission to use the bomb," O'Donnell grumbled. "And I'll get it, but not until after those jackasses end their damned talking." He stopped pacing and turned to Micheals. "I am going to destroy the leech. I am going to smash it, if that's the last thing I do. It's more than a matter of security now. It's personal pride."

That attitude might make great generals, Micheals thought, but it wasn't the way to consider this problem. It was anthropomorphic of

O'Donnell to see the leech as an enemy. Even the identification, "leech," was a humanizing factor. O'Donnell was dealing with it as he would any physical obstacle, as though the leech were the simple equivalent of a large army.

But the leech was not human, not even of this planet, perhaps. It should be dealt with in its own terms.

"Here come the bright boys now," O'Donnell said.

From a nearby tent a group of weary men emerged, led by Allenson, a government biologist.

"Well," the general asked, "have you figured out what it is?"

"Just a minute, I'll hack off a sample," Allenson said, glaring through red-rimmed eyes.

"Have you figured out some scientific way of killing it?"

"Oh, that wasn't too difficult," Moriarty, an atomic physicist, said wryly. "Wrap it in a perfect vacuum. That'll do the trick. Or blow it off the Earth with anti-gravity."

"But failing that," Allenson said, "we suggest you use your atomic bombs, and use them fast."

"Is that the opinion of your entire group?" O'Donnell asked, his eyes glittering.

"Yes."

The general hurried away. Micheals joined the scientists.

"He should have called us in at the very first," Allenson complained. "There's no time to consider anything but force now."

"Have you come to any conclusions about the nature of the leech?" Micheals asked.

"Only general ones," Moriarty said, "and they're about the same as yours. The leech is probably extraterrestrial in origin. It seems to have been in a spore-stage until it landed on Earth." He paused to light a pipe. "Incidentally, we should be damned glad it didn't drop in an ocean. We'd have had the Earth eaten out from under us before we knew what we were looking for."

They walked in silence for a few minutes.

"As you mentioned, it's a perfect converter—it can transform mass into energy, and any energy into mass." Moriarty grinned. "Naturally that's impossible and I have figures to prove it."

"I'm going to get a drink," Allenson said. "Anyone coming?"

"Best idea of the week," Micheals said. "I wonder how long it'll take O'Donnell to get permission to use the bomb."

"If I know politics," Moriarty said, "too long."

The findings of the government scientists were checked by other government scientists. That took a few days. Then Washington wanted to know if there wasn't some alternative to exploding an atomic bomb in the middle of New York State. It took a little time to convince them of the necessity. After that, people had to be evacuated, which took more time.

Then orders were made out, and five atomic bombs were checked out of a cache. A patrol rocket was assigned, given orders, and put under General O'Donnell's command. This took a day more.

Finally, the stubby scout rocket was winging its way over New York. From the air, the grayish-black spot was easy to find. Like a festered wound, it stretched between Lake Placid and Elizabethtown, covering Keene and Keene Valley, and lapping at the edges of Jay.

The first bomb was released.

It had been a long wait after the first rich food. The greater radiation of day was followed by the lesser energy of night many times, as the leech ate away the earth beneath it, absorbed the air around it, and grew. Then one day—

An amazing burst of energy!

Everything was food for the leech, but there was always the possibility of choking. The energy poured over it, drenched it, battered it, and the leech grew frantically, trying to contain the titanic dose. Still small, it quickly reached its overload limit. The strained cells, filled to satiation, were given more and more food. The strangling body built new cells at lightning speed. And—

It held. The energy was controlled, stimulating further growth. More cells took over the load, sucking in the food.

The next doses were wonderfully palatable, easily handled. The leech overflowed its bounds, growing, eating, and growing.

That was a taste of real food! The leech was as near ecstasy as it had ever been. It waited hopefully for more, but no more came.

It went back to feeding on the Earth. The energy, used to produce more cells, was soon dissipated. Soon it was hungry again.

It would always be hungry.

O'Donnell retreated with his demoralized men. They camped ten miles from the leech's southern edge, in the evacuated town of Schroon Lake. The leech was over sixty miles in diameter now and still growing fast. It lay sprawled over the Adirondack Mountains, completely blanketing everything from Saranac Lake to Port Henry, with one edge of it over Westport, in Lake Champlain.

Everyone within two hundred miles of the leech was evacuated.

General O'Donnell was given permission to use hydrogen bombs, contingent on the approval of his scientists.

"What have the bright boys decided?" O'Donnell wanted to know.

He and Micheals were in the living room of an evacuated Schroon Lake house. O'Donnell had made it his new command post.

"Why are they hedging?" O'Donnell demanded impatiently. "The leech has to be blown up quick. What are they fooling around for?"

"They're afraid of a chain reaction," Micheals told him. "A concentration of hydrogen bombs might set one up in the Earth's crust or in the atmosphere. It might do any of half a dozen things."

"Perhaps they'd like me to order a bayonet attack," O'Donnell said contemptuously.

Micheals sighed and sat down in an armchair. He was convinced that the whole method was wrong. The government scientists were being rushed into a single line of inquiry. The pressure on them was so great that they didn't have a chance to consider any other approach but force—and the leech thrived on that.

Micheals was certain that there were times when fighting fire with fire was not applicable.

Fire. Loki, god of fire. And of trickery. No, there was no answer there. But Micheals' mind was in mythology now, retreating from the unbearable present.

Allenson came in, followed by six other men.

"Well," Allenson said, "there's a damned good chance of splitting the Earth wide open if you use the number of bombs our figures show you need."

"You have to take chances in war," O'Donnell replied bluntly. "Shall I go ahead?"

Micheals saw, suddenly, that O'Donnell didn't care if he did crack the Earth. The red-faced general only knew that he was going to set off the greatest explosion ever produced by the hand of Man.

"Not so fast," Allenson said. "I'll let the others speak for themselves."

The general contained himself with difficulty. "Remember," he said, "according to your own figures, the leech is growing at the rate of twenty feet an hour."

"And speeding up," Allenson added. "But this isn't a decision to be made in haste."

Micheals found his mind wandering again, to the lightning bolts of Zeus. That was what they needed. Or the strength of Hercules.

Or—

He sat up suddenly. "Gentlemen, I believe I can offer you a possible alternative, although it's a very dim one."

They stared at him.

"Have you ever heard of Antaeus?" he asked.

The more the leech ate, the faster it grew and the hungrier it became. Although its birth was forgotten, it did remember a long way back. It had eaten a planet in that ancient past. Grown tremendous, ravenous, it had made the journey to a nearby star and eaten that, replenishing the cells converted into energy for the trip. But then there was no more food, and the next star was an enormous distance away.

It set out on the journey, but long before it reached the food, its energy ran out. Mass, converted back to energy to make the trip, was used up. It shrank.

Finally, all the energy was gone. It was a spore, drifting aimlessly, lifelessly, in space.

That was the first time. Or was it? It thought it could remember back to a distant, misty time when the Universe was evenly covered with stars. It had eaten through them, cutting away whole sections, growing, swelling. And the stars had swung off in terror, forming galaxies and constellations.

Or was that a dream?

Methodically, it fed on the Earth, wondering where the rich food was. And then it was back again, but this time above the leech.

It waited, but the tantalizing food remained out of reach. It was able to sense how rich and pure the food was.

Why didn't it fall?

For a long time the leech waited, but the food stayed out of reach. At last, it lifted and followed.

The food retreated, up, up from the surface of the planet. The leech went after as quickly as its bulk would allow.

The rich food fled out, into space, and the leech followed. Beyond, it could sense an even richer source.

The hot, wonderful food of a sun!

O'Donnell served champagne for the scientists in the control room. Official dinners would follow, but this was the victory celebration.

"A toast," the general said, standing. The men raised their glasses. The only man not drinking was a lieutenant, sitting in front of the control board that guided the drone spaceship.

"To Micheals, for thinking of—what was it again, Micheals?"

"Antaeus." Micheals had been drinking champagne steadily, but he didn't feel elated. Antaeus, born of Ge, the Earth, and Poseidon, the Sea. The invincible wrestler. Each time Hercules threw him to the ground, he arose refreshed.

Until Hercules held him in the air.

Moriarty was muttering to himself, figuring with slide rule, pencil and paper. Allenson was drinking, but he didn't look too happy about it.

"Come on, you birds of evil omen," O'Donnell said, pouring more champagne. "Figure it out later. Right now, drink." He turned to the operator. "How's it going?"

Micheals' analogy had been applied to a spaceship. The ship, operated by remote control, was filled with pure radioactives. It hovered over the leech until, rising to the bait, it had followed. Antaeus had left his mother, the Earth, and was losing his strength in the air. The operator was allowing the spaceship to run fast enough to keep out of the leech's grasp, but close enough to keep it coming.

The spaceship and the leech were on a collision course with the Sun.

"Fine, sir," the operator said. "It's inside the orbit of Mercury now."

"Men," the general said, "I swore to destroy that thing. This isn't exactly the way I wanted to do it. I figured on a more personal way. But the important thing is the destruction. You will all witness it. Destruction is at times a sacred mission. This is such a time. Men, I feel wonderful."

"Turn the spaceship!" It was Moriarty who had spoken. His face was white. "Turn the damned thing!"

He shoved his figures at them.

They were easy to read. The growth-rate of the leech. The energy-consumption rate, estimated. Its speed in space, a constant. The energy it would receive from the Sun as it approached, an exponential curve. Its energy-absorption rate, figured in terms of growth, expressed as a hyped-up discontinuous progression.

The result—

"It'll consume the Sun," Moriarty said, very quietly.

The control room turned into a bedlam. Six of them tried to explain it to O'Donnell at the same time. Then Moriarty tried, and finally Allenson.

"Its rate of growth is so great and its speed so slow—and it will get so much energy—that the leech will be able to consume the Sun by the time it gets there. Or, at least, to live off it until it can consume it."

O'Donnell didn't bother to understand. He turned to the operator.

"Turn it," he said.

They all hovered over the radar screen, waiting.

The food turned out of the leech's path and streaked away. Ahead was a tremendous source, but still a long way off. The leech hesitated.

Its cells, recklessly expending energy, shouted for a decision. The food slowed, tantalizingly near.

The closer source or the greater?

The leech's body wanted food now.

It started after it, away from the Sun.

The Sun would come next.

"Pull it out at right angles to the plane of the Solar System," Allenson said.

The operator touched the controls. On the radar screen, they saw a blob pursuing a dot. It had turned.

Relief washed over them. It had been close!

"In what portion of the sky would the leech be?" O'Donnell asked, his face expressionless.

"Come outside; I believe I can show you," an astronomer said. They walked to the door. "Somewhere in that section," the astronomer said, pointing.

"Fine. All right, Soldier," O'Donnell told the operator. "Carry out your orders."

The scientists gasped in unison. The operator manipulated the controls and the blob began to overtake the dot. Micheals started across the room.

"Stop," the general said, and his strong, commanding voice stopped Micheals. "I know what I'm doing. I had that ship especially built."

The blob overtook the dot on the radar screen.

"I told you this was a personal matter," O'Donnell said. "I swore to destroy that leech. We can never have any security while it lives." He smiled. "Shall we look at the sky?"

The general strolled to the door, followed by the scientists.

"Push the button, Soldier!"

The operator did. For a moment, nothing happened. Then the sky lit up!

A bright star hung in space. Its brilliance filled the night, grew, and started to fade.

"What did you do?" Micheals gasped.

"That rocket was built around a hydrogen bomb," O'Donnell said, his strong face triumphant. "I set it off at the contact moment." He called to the operator again. "Is there anything showing on the radar?"

"Not a speck, sir."

"Men," the general said, "I have met the enemy and he is mine. Let's have some more champagne."

But Micheals found that he was suddenly ill.

It had been shrinking from the expenditure of energy, when the great explosion came. No thought of containing it. The leech's cells held for the barest fraction of a second, and then spontaneously overloaded.

The leech was smashed, broken up, destroyed. It was split into a thousand particles, and the particles were split a million times more.

The particles were thrown out on the wave front of the explosion, and they split further, spontaneously.

Into spores.

The spores closed into dry, hard, seemingly lifeless specks of dust, billions of them, scattered, drifting. Unconscious, they floated in the emptiness of space.

Billions of them, waiting to be fed.

WARRIOR RACE

Illustrated by SCATTERGOOD

Destroying the spirit of the enemy is the goal of war and the aliens had the best way!

They never did discover whose fault it was. Fannia pointed out that if Donnaught had had the brains of an ox, as well as the build, he would have remembered to check the tanks. Donnaught, although twice as big as him, wasn't quite as fast with an insult. He intimated, after a little thought, that Fannia's nose might have obstructed his reading of the fuel gauge.

This still left them twenty light-years from Thetis, with a cupful of transformer fuel in the emergency tank.

"All right," Fannia said presently. "What's done is done. We can squeeze about three light-years out of the fuel before we're back on atomics. Hand me The Galactic Pilot—unless you forgot that, too."

Donnaught dragged the bulky microfilm volume out of its locker, and they explored its pages.

The Galactic Pilot told them they were in a sparse, seldom-visited section of space, which they already knew. The nearest planetary system was Hatterfield; no intelligent life there. Sersus had a native population, but no refueling facilities. The same with Illed, Hung and Porderai.

"Ah-ha!" Fannia said. "Read that, Donnaught. If you can read, that is."

"Cascella," Donnaught read, slowly and clearly, following the line with a thick forefinger. "Type M sun. Three planets, intelligent (AA3C) human-type life on second. Oxygen-breathers. Non-mechanical. Religious. Friendly. Unique social structure, described in Galactic Survey Report 33877242. Population estimate: stable at three billion. Basic Cascellan vocabulary taped under Cas33b2. Scheduled for resurvey 2375 A.D. Cache of transformer fuel left, beam coordinate 8741 kgl. Physical descript: Unocc. flatland."

"Transformer fuel, boy!" Fannia said gleefully. "I believe we will get to Thetis, after all." He punched the new direction on the ship's tape. "If that fuel's still there."

"Should we read up on the unique social structure?" Donnaught asked, still poring over The Galactic Pilot.

"Certainly," Fannia said. "Just step over to the main galactic base on Earth and buy me a copy."

"I forgot," Donnaught admitted slowly.

"Let me see," Fannia said, dragging out the ship's language library,

"Cascellan, Cascellan ... Here it is. Be good while I learn the language." He set the tape in the hypnophone and switched it on. "Another useless tongue in my overstuffed head," he murmured, and then the hypnophone took over.

Coming out of transformer drive with at least a drop of fuel left, they switched to atomics. Fannia rode the beam right across the planet, locating the slender metal spire of the Galactic Survey cache. The plain was no longer unoccupied, however. The Cascellans had built a city around the cache, and the spire dominated the crude wood-and-mud buildings.

"Hang on," Fannia said, and brought the ship down on the outskirts of the city, in a field of stubble.

"Now look," Fannia said, unfastening his safety belt. "We're just here for fuel. No souvenirs, no side-trips, no fraternizing."

Through the port, they could see a cloud of dust from the city. As it came closer, they made out figures running toward their ship.

"What do you think this unique social structure is?" Donnaught asked, pensively checking the charge in a needler gun.

"I know not and care less," Fannia said, struggling into space armor. "Get dressed."

"The air's breathable."

"Look, pachyderm, for all we know, these Cascellans think the proper way to greet visitors is to chop off their heads and stuff them with green apples. If Galactic says unique, it probably means unique."

"Galactic said they were friendly."

"That means they haven't got atomic bombs. Come on, get dressed." Donnaught put down the needler and struggled into an oversize suit of space armor. Both men strapped on needlers, paralyzers, and a few grenades.

"I don't think we have anything to worry about," Fannia said, tightening the last nut on his helmet. "Even if they get rough, they can't crack space armor. And if they're not rough, we won't have any trouble. Maybe these gewgaws will help." He picked up a box of trading articles—mirrors, toys and the like.

Helmeted and armored, Fannia slid out the port and raised one hand to the Cascellans. The language, hypnotically placed in his mind, leaped to his lips.

"We come as friends and brothers. Take us to the chief."

The natives clustered around, gaping at the ship and the space armor. Although they had the same number of eyes, ears and limbs as humans, they completely missed looking like them.

"If they're friendly," Donnaught asked, climbing out of the port, "why all the hardware?" The Cascellans were dressed predominantly in a collection of knives, swords and daggers. Each man had at least five, and some had eight or nine.

"Maybe Galactic got their signals crossed," Fannia said, as the natives spread out in an escort. "Or maybe the natives just use the knives for mumblypeg."

The city was typical of a non-mechanical culture. Narrow, packed-dirt streets twisted between ramshackle huts. A few two-story buildings threatened to collapse at any minute. A stench filled the air, so strong that Fannia's filter couldn't quite eradicate it. The Cascellans bounded ahead of the heavily laden Earthmen, dashing around like a pack of playful puppies. Their knives glittered and clanked.

The chief's house was the only three-story building in the city. The tall spire of the cache was right behind it.

"If you come in peace," the chief said when they entered, "you are welcome." He was a middle-aged Cascellan with at least fifteen knives strapped to various parts of his person. He squatted cross-legged on a raised dais.

"We are privileged," Fannia said. He remembered from the hypnotic language lesson that "chief" on Cascella meant more than it usually did on Earth. The chief here was a combination of king, high priest, deity and bravest warrior.

"We have a few simple gifts here," Fannia added, placing the gewgaws at the king's feet. "Will his majesty accept?"

"No," the king said. "We accept no gifts." Was that the unique social structure? Fannia wondered. It certainly was not human. "We are a warrior race. What we want, we take."

Fannia sat cross-legged in front of the dais and exchanged conversation with the king while Donnaught played with the spurned toys. Trying to overcome the initial bad impression, Fannia told the chief about the stars and other worlds, since simple people usually liked fables. He spoke of the ship, not mentioning yet that it was out of fuel. He spoke of Cascella, telling the chief how its fame was known throughout the Galaxy.

"That is as it should be," the chief said proudly. "We are a race of warriors, the like of which has never been seen. Every man of us dies fighting."

"You must have fought some great wars," Fannia said politely, wondering what idiot had written up the galactic report.

"I have not fought a war for many years," the chief said. "We are united now, and all our enemies have joined us."

Bit by bit, Fannia led up to the matter of the fuel.

"What is this 'fuel'?" the chief asked, haltingly because there was no equivalent for it in the Cascellan language.

"It makes our ship go."

"And where is it?"

"In the metal spire," Fannia said. "If you would just allow us—"

"In the holy shrine?" the chief exclaimed, shocked. "The tall metal church which the gods left here long ago?"

"Yeah," Fannia said sadly, knowing what was coming. "I guess that's it."

"It is sacrilege for an outworlder to go near it," the chief said. "I forbid it."

"We need the fuel." Fannia was getting tired of sitting cross-legged. Space armor wasn't built for complicated postures. "The spire was put here for such emergencies."

"Strangers, know that I am god of my people, as well as their leader. If you dare approach the sacred temple, there will be war."

"I was afraid of that," Fannia said, getting to his feet.

"And since we are a race of warriors," the chief said, "at my command, every fighting man of the planet will move against you. More will come from the hills and from across the rivers."

Abruptly, the chief drew a knife. It must have been a signal, because every native in the room did the same.

Fannia dragged Donnaught away from the toys. "Look, lummox. These friendly warriors can't do a damn thing to us. Those knives can't cut space armor, and I doubt if they have anything better. Don't let them pile up on you, though. Use the paralyzer first, the needler if they really get thick."

"Right." Donnaught whisked out and primed a paralyzer in a single coordinated movement. With weapons, Donnaught was fast and reliable, which was virtue enough for Fannia to keep him as a partner.

"We'll cut around this building and grab the fuel. Two cans ought to be enough. Then we'll beat it fast."

They walked out the building, followed by the Cascellans. Four carriers lifted the chief, who was barking orders. The narrow street outside was suddenly jammed with armed natives. No one tried to touch them yet, but at least a thousand knives were flashing in the sun.

In front of the cache was a solid phalanx of Cascellans. They stood behind a network of ropes that probably marked the boundary between sacred and profane ground.

"Get set for it," Fannia said, and stepped over the ropes.

Immediately the foremost temple guard raised his knife. Fannia brought up the paralyzer, not firing it yet, still moving forward.

The foremost native shouted something, and the knife swept across in a glittering arc. The Cascellan gurgled something else, staggered and fell. Bright blood oozed from his throat.

"I told you not to use the needler yet!" Fannia said.

"I didn't," Donnaught protested. Glancing back, Fannia saw that Donnaught's needler was still holstered.

"Then I don't get it," said Fannia bewilderedly.

Three more natives bounded forward, their knives held high. They tumbled to the ground also. Fannia stopped and watched as a platoon of natives advanced on them.

Once they were within stabbing range of the Earthmen, the natives were slitting their own throats!

Fannia was frozen for a moment, unable to believe his eyes. Donnaught halted behind him.

Natives were rushing forward by the hundreds now, their knives poised, screaming at the Earthmen. As they came within range, each native stabbed himself, tumbling on a quickly growing pile of bodies. In minutes the Earthmen were surrounded by a heap of bleeding Cascellan flesh, which was steadily growing higher.

"All right!" Fannia shouted. "Stop it." He yanked Donnaught back with him, to profane ground. "Truce!" he yelled in Cascellan.

The crowd parted and the chief was carried through. With two knives clenched in his fists, he was panting from excitement.

"We have won the first battle!" he said proudly. "The might of our warriors frightens even such aliens as yourselves. You shall not profane our temple while a man is alive on Cascella!"

The natives shouted their approval and triumph.

The two aliens dazedly stumbled back to their ship.

"So that's what Galactic meant by 'a unique social structure,'" Fannia said morosely. He stripped off his armor and lay down on his bunk. "Their way of making war is to suicide their enemies into capitulation."

"They must be nuts," Donnaught grumbled. "That's no way to fight."

"It works, doesn't it?" Fannia got up and stared out a porthole. The sun was setting, painting the city a charming red in its glow. The beams of light glistened off the spire of the Galactic cache. Through the open doorway they could hear the boom and rattle of drums. "Tribal call to arms," Fannia said.

"I still say it's crazy." Donnaught had some definite ideas on fighting. "It ain't human."

"I'll buy that. The idea seems to be that if enough people slaughter themselves, the enemy gives up out of sheer guilty conscience."

"What if the enemy doesn't give up?"

"Before these people united, they must have fought it out tribe to tribe, suiciding until someone gave up. The losers probably joined the victors; the tribe must have grown until it could take over the planet by sheer weight of numbers." Fannia looked carefully at Donnaught, trying to see if he understood. "It's anti-survival, of course; if someone didn't give up, the race would probably kill themselves." He shook his head. "But war of any kind is anti-survival. Perhaps they've got rules."

"Couldn't we just barge in and grab the fuel quick?" Donnaught asked. "And get out before they all killed themselves?"

"I don't think so," Fannia said. "They might go on committing suicide for the next ten years, figuring they were still fighting us." He looked thoughtfully at the city. "It's that chief of theirs. He's their god and he'd probably keep them suiciding until he was the only man left. Then he'd grin, say, 'We are great warriors,' and kill himself."

Donnaught shrugged his big shoulders in disgust. "Why don't we knock him off?"

"They'd just elect another god." The sun was almost below the horizon now. "I've got an idea, though," Fannia said. He scratched his head. "It might work. All we can do is try."

At midnight, the two men sneaked out of the ship, moving silently into the city. They were both dressed in space armor again. Donnaught carried two empty fuel cans. Fannia had his paralyzer out.

The streets were dark and silent as they slid along walls and around posts, keeping out of sight. A native turned a corner suddenly, but Fannia paralyzed him before he could make a sound.

They crouched in the darkness, in the mouth of an alley facing the cache.

"Have you got it straight?" Fannia asked. "I paralyze the guards. You bolt in and fill up those cans. We get the hell out of here, quick. When they check, they find the cans still there. Maybe they won't commit suicide then."

The men moved across the shadowy steps in front of the cache. There were three Cascellans guarding the entrance, their knives stuck in their loincloths. Fannia stunned them with a medium charge, and Donnaught broke into a run.

Torches instantly flared, natives boiled out of every alleyway, shouting, waving their knives.

"We've been ambushed!" Fannia shouted. "Get back here, Donnaught!"

Donnaught hurriedly retreated. The natives had been waiting for them.

Screaming, yowling, they rushed at the Earthmen, slitting their own throats at five-foot range. Bodies tumbled in front of Fannia, almost tripping him as he backed up. Donnaught caught him by an arm and yanked him straight. They ran out of the sacred area.

"Truce, damn it!" Fannia called out. "Let me speak to the chief. Stop it! Stop it! I want a truce!"

Reluctantly, the Cascellans stopped their slaughter.

"This is war," the chief said, striding forward. His almost human face was stern under the torchlight. "You have seen our warriors. You know now that you cannot stand against them. The word has spread to all our lands. My entire people are prepared to do battle."

He looked proudly at his fellow-Cascellans, then back to the Earthmen. "I myself will lead my people into battle now. There will be no stopping us. We will fight until you surrender yourselves completely, stripping off your armor."

"Wait, Chief," Fannia panted, sick at the sight of so much blood. The clearing was a scene out of the Inferno. Hundreds of bodies were sprawled around. The streets were muddy with blood.

"Let me confer with my partner tonight. I will speak with you tomorrow."

"No," the chief said. "You started the battle. It must go to its conclusion. Brave men wish to die in battle. It is our fondest wish. You are the first enemy we have had in many years, since we subdued the mountain tribes."

"Sure," Fannia said. "But let's talk about it—"

"I myself will fight you," the chief said, holding up a dagger. "I will die for my people, as a warrior must!"

"Hold it!" Fannia shouted. "Grant us a truce. We are allowed to fight only by sunlight. It is a tribal taboo."

The chief thought for a moment, then said, "Very well. Until tomorrow."

The beaten Earthmen walked slowly back to their ship amid the jeers of the victorious populace.

Next morning, Fannia still didn't have a plan. He knew that he had to have fuel; he wasn't planning on spending the rest of his life on Cascella, or waiting until the Galactic Survey sent another ship, in fifty years or so. On the other hand, he hesitated at the idea of being responsible for the death of anywhere up to three billion people. It wouldn't be a very good record to take to Thetis. The Galactic Survey might find out about it. Anyway, he just wouldn't do it.

He was stuck both ways.

Slowly, the two men walked out to meet the chief. Fannia was still searching wildly for an idea while listening to the drums booming.

"If there was only someone we could fight," Donnaught mourned, looking at his useless blasters.

"That's the deal," Fannia said. "Guilty conscience is making sinners of us all, or something like that. They expect us to give in before the carnage gets out of hand." He considered for a moment. "It's not so crazy, actually. On Earth, armies don't usually fight until every last man is slaughtered on one side. Someone surrenders when they've had enough."

"If they'd just fight us!"

"Yeah, if they only—" He stopped. "We'll fight each other!" he said. "These people look at suicide as war. Wouldn't they look upon war—real fighting—as suicide?"

"What good would that do us?" Donnaught asked.

They were coming into the city now and the streets were lined with armed natives. Around the city there were thousands more. Natives were filling the plain, as far as the eye could see. Evidently they had responded to the drums and were here to do battle with the aliens.

Which meant, of course, a wholesale suicide.

"Look at it this way," Fannia said. "If a guy plans on suiciding on Earth, what do we do?"

"Arrest him?" Donnaught asked.

"Not at first. We offer him anything he wants, if he just won't do it. People offer the guy money, a job, their daughters, anything, just so he won't do it. It's taboo on Earth."

"So?"

"So," Fannia went on, "maybe fighting is just as taboo here. Maybe they'll offer us fuel, if we'll just stop."

Donnaught looked dubious, but Fannia felt it was worth a try.

They pushed their way through the crowded city, to the entrance of the cache. The chief was waiting for them, beaming on his people like a jovial war god.

"Are you ready to do battle?" he asked. "Or to surrender?"

"Sure," Fannia said. "Now, Donnaught!"

He swung, and his mailed fist caught Donnaught in the ribs. Donnaught blinked.

"Come on, you idiot, hit me back."

Donnaught swung, and Fannia staggered from the force of the blow. In a second they were at it like a pair of blacksmiths, mailed blows ringing from their armored hides.

"A little lighter," Fannia gasped, picking himself up from the ground. "You're denting my ribs." He belted Donnaught viciously on the helmet.

"Stop it!" the chief cried. "This is disgusting!"

"It's working," Fannia panted. "Now let me strangle you. I think that might do it."

Donnaught obliged by falling to the ground. Fannia clamped both hands around Donnaught's armored neck, and squeezed.

"Make believe you're in agony, idiot," he said.

Donnaught groaned and moaned as convincingly as he could.

"You must stop!" the chief screamed. "It is terrible to kill another!"

"Then let me get some fuel," Fannia said, tightening his grip on Donnaught's throat.

The chief thought it over for a little while. Then he shook his head. "No."

"What?"

"You are aliens. If you want to do this disgraceful thing, do it. But you shall not profane our religious relics."

———————————

Donnaught and Fannia staggered to their feet. Fannia was exhausted from fighting in the heavy space armor; he barely made it up.

"Now," the chief said, "surrender at once. Take off your armor or do battle with us."

The thousands of warriors—possibly millions, because more were arriving every second—shouted their blood-wrath. The cry was taken up on the outskirts and echoed to the hills, where more fighting men were pouring down into the crowded plain.

Fannia's face contorted. He couldn't give himself and Donnaught up to the Cascellans. They might be cooked at the next church supper. For a moment he considered going after the fuel and letting the damned fools suicide all they pleased.

His mind an angry blank, Fannia staggered forward and hit the chief in the face with a mailed glove.

The chief went down, and the natives backed away in horror. Quickly, the chief snapped out a knife and brought it up to his throat. Fannia's hands closed on the chief's wrists.

"Listen to me," Fannia croaked. "We're going to take that fuel. If any man makes a move—if anyone kills himself—I'll kill your chief."

The natives milled around uncertainly. The chief was struggling wildly in Fannia's hands, trying to get a knife to his throat, so he could die honorably.

"Get it," Fannia told Donnaught, "and hurry it up."

The natives were uncertain just what to do. They had their knives poised at their throats, ready to plunge if battle was joined.

"Don't do it," Fannia warned. "I'll kill the chief and then he'll never die a warrior's death."

The chief was still trying to kill himself. Desperately, Fannia held on, knowing he had to keep him from suicide in order to hold the threat of death over him.

"Listen, Chief," Fannia said, eying the uncertain crowd. "I must have your promise there'll be no more war between us. Either I get it or I kill you."

"Warriors!" the chief roared. "Choose a new ruler. Forget me and do battle!"

The Cascellans were still uncertain, but knives started to lift.

"If you do it," Fannia shouted in despair, "I'll kill your chief. I'll kill all of you!"

That stopped them.

"I have powerful magic in my ship. I can kill every last man, and then you won't be able to die a warrior's death. Or get to heaven!"

The chief tried to free himself with a mighty surge that almost tore one of his arms free, but Fannia held on, pinning both arms behind his back.

"Very well," the chief said, tears springing into his eyes. "A warrior must die by his own hand. You have won, alien."

The crowd shouted curses as the Earthmen carried the chief and the cans of fuel back to the ship. They waved their knives and danced up and down in a frenzy of hate.

"Let's make it fast," Fannia said, after Donnaught had fueled the ship.

He gave the chief a push and leaped in. In a second they were in the air, heading for Thetis and the nearest bar at top speed.

The natives were hot for blood—their own. Every man of them pledged his life to wiping out the insult to their leader and god, and to their shrine.

But the aliens were gone. There was nobody to fight.

THE HOUR OF BATTLE

ILLUSTRATED BY KRENKEL

As one of the Guardian ships protecting Earth, the crew had a problem to solve. Just how do you protect a race from an enemy who can take over a man's mind without seeming effort or warning?

"That hand didn't move, did it?" Edwardson asked, standing at the port, looking at the stars.

"No," Morse said. He had been staring fixedly at the Attison Detector for over an hour. Now he blinked three times rapidly, and looked again. "Not a millimeter."

"I don't think it moved either," Cassel added, from behind the gunfire panel. And that was that. The slender black hand of the indicator rested unwaveringly on zero. The ship's guns were ready, their black mouths open to the stars. A steady hum filled the room. It came from the Attison Detector, and the sound was reassuring. It reinforced the fact that the Detector was attached to all the other Detectors, forming a gigantic network around Earth.

"Why in hell don't they come?" Edwardson asked, still looking at the stars. "Why don't they hit?"

"Aah, shut up," Morse said. He had a tired, glum look. High on his right temple was an old radiation burn, a sunburst of pink scar tissue. From a distance it looked like a decoration.

"I just wish they'd come," Edwardson said. He returned from the port to his chair, bending to clear the low metal ceiling. "Don't you wish they'd come?" Edwardson had the narrow, timid face of a mouse; but a highly intelligent mouse. One that cats did well to avoid.

"Don't you?" he repeated.

The other men didn't answer. They had settled back to their dreams, staring hypnotically at the Detector face.

"They've had enough time," Edwardson said, half to himself.

Cassel yawned and licked his lips. "Anyone want to play some gin?" he asked, stroking his beard. The beard was a memento of his undergraduate days. Cassel maintained he could store almost fifteen minutes worth of oxygen in its follicles. He had never stepped into space unhelmeted to prove it.

Morse looked away, and Edwardson automatically watched the indicator. This routine had been drilled into them, branded into their subconscious. They would as soon have cut their throats as leave the indicator unguarded.

"Do you think they'll come soon?" Edwardson asked, his brown rodent's eyes on the indicator. The men didn't answer him. After two months together in space their conversational powers were exhausted. They weren't interested in Cassel's undergraduate days, or in Morse's conquests.

They were bored to death even with their own thoughts and dreams, bored with the attack they expected momentarily.

"Just one thing I'd like to know," Edwardson said, slipping with ease into an old conversational gambit. "How far can they do it?"

They had talked for weeks about the enemy's telepathic range, but they always returned to it.

As professional soldiers, they couldn't help but speculate on the enemy and his weapons. It was their shop talk.

"Well," Morse said wearily, "Our Detector network covers the system out beyond Mars' orbit."

"Where we sit," Cassel said, watching the indicators now that the others were talking.

"They might not even know we have a detection unit working," Morse said, as he had said a thousand times.

"Oh, stop," Edwardson said, his thin face twisted in scorn. "They're telepathic. They must have read every bit of stuff in Everset's mind."

"Everset didn't know we had a detection unit," Morse said, his eyes returning to the dial. "He was captured before we had it."

"Look," Edwardson said, "They ask him, 'Boy, what would you do if you knew a telepathic race was coming to take over Earth? How would you guard the planet?'"

"Idle speculation," Cassel said. "Maybe Everset

didn't think of this."

"He thinks like a man, doesn't he? Everyone agreed on this defense. Everset would, too."

"Syllogistic," Cassel murmured. "Very shaky."

"I sure wish he hadn't been captured," Edwardson said.

"It could have been worse," Morse put in, his face sadder than ever. "What if they'd captured both of them?"

"I wish they'd come," Edwardson said.

Richard Everset and C. R. Jones had gone on the first interstellar flight. They had found an inhabited planet in the region of Vega. The rest was standard procedure.

A flip of the coin had decided it. Everset went down in the scouter, maintaining radio contact with Jones, in the ship.

The recording of that contact was preserved for all Earth to hear.

"Just met the natives," Everset said. "Funny-looking bunch. Give you the physical description later."

"Are they trying to talk to you?" Jones asked, guiding the ship in a slow spiral over the planet.

"No. Hold it. Well I'm damned! They're telepathic! How do you like that?"

"Great," Jones said. "Go on."

"Hold it. Say, Jonesy, I don't know as I like these boys. They haven't got nice minds. Brother!"

"What is it?" Jones asked, lifting the ship a little higher.

"Minds! These bastards are power-crazy. Seems they've hit all the systems around here, looking for someone to—"

"Yeh?"

"I've got that a bit wrong," Everset said pleasantly. "They are not so bad."

Jones had a quick mind, a suspicious nature and good reflexes. He set the accelerator for all the G's he could take, lay down on the floor and said, "Tell me more."

"Come on down," Everset said, in violation of every law of spaceflight. "These guys are all right. As a matter of fact, they're the most marvelous—"

That was where the recording ended, because Jones was pinned to the floor by twenty G's acceleration as he boosted the ship to the level needed for the C-jump.

He broke three ribs getting home, but he got there.

A telepathic species was on the march. What was Earth going to do about it?

A lot of speculation necessarily clothed the bare bones of Jones' information. Evidently the species could take over a mind with ease. With Everset, it seemed that they had insinuated their thoughts into his, delicately altering his previous convictions. They had possessed him with remarkable ease.

How about Jones? Why hadn't they taken him? Was distance a factor? Or hadn't they been prepared for the suddenness of his departure?

One thing was certain. Everything Everset knew, the enemy knew. That meant they knew where Earth was, and how defenseless the planet was to their form of attack.

It could be expected that they were on their way.

Something was needed to nullify their tremendous advantage. But what sort of something? What armor is there against thought? How do you dodge a wavelength?

Pouch-eyed scientists gravely consulted their periodic tables.

And how do you know when a man has been possessed? Although the enemy was clumsy with Everset, would they continue to be clumsy? Wouldn't they learn?

Psychologists tore their hair and bewailed the absence of an absolute scale for humanity.

Of course, something had to be done at once. The answer, from a technological planet, was a technological one. Build a space fleet and equip it with some sort of a detection-fire network.

This was done in record time. The Attison Detector was developed, a cross between radar and the electroencephalograph. Any alteration from the typical human brain wave pattern of the occupants of a Detector-equipped ship would boost the indicator around the dial. Even a bad dream or a case of indigestion would jar it.

It seemed probable that any attempt to take over a human mind would disturb something. There had to be a point of interaction, somewhere.

That was what the Attison Detector was supposed to detect. Maybe it would.

The spaceships, three men to a ship, dotted space between Earth and Mars, forming a gigantic sphere with Earth in the center.

Tens of thousands of men crouched behind gunfire panels, watching the dials on the Attison Detector.

The unmoving dials.

"Do you think I could fire a couple of bursts?" Edwardson asked, his fingers on the gunfire button. "Just to limber the guns?"

"Those guns don't need limbering," Cassel said, stroking his beard. "Besides, you'd throw the whole fleet into a panic."

"Cassel," Morse said, very quietly. "Get your hand off your beard."

"Why should I?" Cassel asked.

"Because," Morse answered, almost in a whisper, "I am about to ram it right down your fat throat."

Cassel grinned and tightened his fists. "Pleasure," he said. "I'm tired of looking at that scar of yours." He stood up.

"Cut it," Edwardson said wearily. "Watch the birdie."

"No reason to, really," Morse said, leaning back. "There's an alarm bell attached." But he looked at the dial.

"What if the bell doesn't work?" Edwardson asked. "What if the dial is jammed? How would you like something cold slithering into your mind?"

"The dial'll work," Cassel said. His eyes shifted from Edwardson's face to the motionless indicator.

"I think I'll sack in," Edwardson said.

"Stick around," Cassel said. "Play you some gin."

"All right." Edwardson found and shuffled the greasy cards, while Morse took a turn glaring at the dial.

"I sure wish they'd come," he said.

"Cut," Edwardson said, handing the pack to Cassel.

"I wonder what our friends look like," Morse said, watching the dial.

"Probably remarkably like us," Edwardson said, dealing the cards. Cassel picked them up one by one, slowly, as if he hoped something interesting would be under them.

"They should have given us another man," Cassel said. "We could play bridge."

"I don't play bridge," Edwardson said.

"You could learn."

"Why didn't we send a task force?" Morse asked. "Why didn't we bomb their planet?"

"Don't be dumb," Edwardson said. "We'd lose any ship we sent. Probably get them back at us, possessed and firing."

"Knock with nine," Cassel said.

"I don't give a good damn if you knock with a thousand," Edwardson said gaily. "How much do I owe you now?"

"Three million five hundred and eight thousand and ten. Dollars."

"I sure wish they'd come," Morse said.

"Want me to write a check?"

"Take your time. Take until next week."

"Someone should reason with the bastards," Morse said, looking out the port. Cassel immediately looked at the dial.

"I just thought of something," Edwardson said.

"Yeh?"

"I bet it feels horrible to have your mind grabbed," Edwardson said. "I bet it's awful."

"You'll know when it happens," Cassel said.

"Did Everset?"

"Probably. He just couldn't do anything about it."

"My mind feels fine," Cassel said. "But the first one of you guys starts acting queer—watch out."

They all laughed.

"Well," Edwardson said, "I'd sure like a chance to reason with them. This is stupid."

"Why not?" Cassel asked.

"You mean go out and meet them?"

"Sure," Cassel said. "We're doing no good sitting here."

"I should think we could do something," Edwardson said slowly. "After all, they're not invincible. They're reasoning beings."

Morse punched a course on the ship's tape, then looked up.

"You think we should contact the command? Tell them what we're doing?"

"No!" Cassel said, and Edwardson nodded in agreement. "Red tape. We'll just go out and see what we can do. If they won't talk, we'll blast 'em out of space."

"Look!"

Out of the port they could see the red flare of a reaction engine; the next ship in their sector, speeding forward.

"They must have got the same idea," Edwardson said.

"Let's get there first," Cassel said. Morse shoved the accelerator in and they were thrown back in their seats.

"That dial hasn't moved yet, has it?" Edwardson asked, over the clamor of the Detector alarm bell.

"Not a move out of it," Cassel said, looking at the dial with its indicator slammed all the way over to the highest notch.

One Man's Poison

Illustrated by EMSH

They could eat a horse, only luckily there was none ... it might have eaten them first!

Hellman plucked the last radish out of the can with a pair of dividers. He held it up for Casker to admire, then laid it carefully on the workbench beside the razor.

"Hell of a meal for two grown men," Casker said, flopping down in one of the ship's padded crash chairs.

"If you'd like to give up your share—" Hellman started to suggest.

Casker shook his head quickly. Hellman smiled, picked up the razor and examined its edge critically.

"Don't make a production out of it," Casker said, glancing at the ship's instruments. They were approaching a red dwarf, the only planet-bearing sun in the vicinity. "We want to be through with supper before we get much closer."

Hellman made a practice incision in the radish, squinting along the top of the razor. Casker bent closer, his mouth open. Hellman poised the razor delicately and cut the radish cleanly in half.

"Will you say grace?" Hellman asked.

Casker growled something and popped a half in his mouth. Hellman chewed more slowly. The sharp taste seemed to explode along his disused tastebuds.

"Not much bulk value," Hellman said.

Casker didn't answer. He was busily studying the red dwarf.

As he swallowed the last of his radish, Hellman stifled a sigh. Their last meal had been three days ago ... if two biscuits and a cup of water could be called a meal. This radish, now resting in the vast emptiness of their stomachs, was the last gram of food on board ship.

"Two planets," Casker said. "One's burned to a crisp."

"Then we'll land on the other."

Casker nodded and punched a deceleration spiral into the ship's tape.

Hellman found himself wondering for the hundredth time where the fault had been. Could he have made out the food requisitions wrong, when they took on supplies at Calao station? After all, he had been devoting most of his attention to the mining equipment. Or had the ground crew just forgotten to load those last precious cases?

He drew his belt in to the fourth new notch he had punched.

Speculation was useless. Whatever the reason, they were in a jam. Ironically enough, they had more than enough fuel to take them back to Calao. But they would be a pair of singularly emaciated corpses by the time the ship reached there.

"We're coming in now," Casker said.

And to make matters worse, this unexplored region of space had few suns and fewer planets. Perhaps there was a slight possibility of replenishing their water supply, but the odds were enormous against finding anything they could eat.

"Look at that place," Casker growled.

Hellman shook himself out of his reverie.

The planet was like a round gray-brown porcupine. The spines of a million needle-sharp mountains glittered in the red dwarf's feeble light. And as they spiraled lower, circling the planet, the pointed mountains seemed to stretch out to meet them.

"It can't be all mountains," Hellman said.

"It's not."

Sure enough, there were oceans and lakes, out of which thrust jagged island-mountains. But no sign of level land, no hint of civilization, or even animal life.

"At least it's got an oxygen atmosphere," Casker said.

Their deceleration spiral swept them around the planet, cutting lower into the atmosphere, braking against it. And still there was nothing but mountains and lakes and oceans and more mountains.

On the eighth run, Hellman caught sight of a solitary building on a mountain top. Casker braked recklessly, and the hull glowed red hot. On the eleventh run, they made a landing approach.

"Stupid place to build," Casker muttered.

The building was doughnut-shaped, and fitted nicely over the top of the mountain. There was a wide, level lip around it, which Casker scorched as he landed the ship.

From the air, the building had merely seemed big. On the ground, it was enormous. Hellman and Casker walked up to it slowly. Hellman had his burner ready, but there was no sign of life.

"This planet must be abandoned," Hellman said almost in a whisper.

"Anyone in his right mind would abandon this place," Casker said. "There're enough good planets around, without anyone trying to live on a needle point."

They reached the door. Hellman tried to open it and found it locked. He looked back at the spectacular display of mountains.

"You know," he said, "when this planet was still in a molten state, it must have been affected by several gigantic moons that are now broken up. The strains, external and internal, wrenched it into its present spined appearance and—"

"Come off it," Casker said ungraciously. "You were a librarian before you decided to get rich on uranium."

Hellman shrugged his shoulders and burned a hole in the doorlock. They waited.

The only sound on the mountain top was the growling of their stomachs.

They entered.

The tremendous wedge-shaped room was evidently a warehouse of sorts. Goods were piled to the ceiling, scattered over the floor, stacked haphazardly against the walls. There were boxes and containers of all sizes and shapes, some big enough to hold an elephant, others the size of thimbles.

Near the door was a dusty pile of books. Immediately, Hellman bent down to examine them.

"Must be food somewhere in here," Casker said, his face lighting up for the first time in a week. He started to open the nearest box.

"This is interesting," Hellman said, discarding all the books except one.

"Let's eat first," Casker said, ripping the top off the box. Inside was a brownish dust. Casker looked at it, sniffed, and made a face.

"Very interesting indeed," Hellman said, leafing through the book.

Casker opened a small can, which contained a glittering green slime. He closed it and opened another. It contained a dull orange slime.

"Hmm," Hellman said, still reading.

"Hellman! Will you kindly drop that book and help me find some food?"

"Food?" Hellman repeated, looking up. "What makes you think there's anything to eat here? For all you know, this could be a paint factory."

"It's a warehouse!" Casker shouted.

He opened a kidney-shaped can and lifted out a soft purple stick. It hardened quickly and crumpled to dust as he tried to smell it. He scooped up a handful of the dust and brought it to his mouth.

"That might be extract of strychnine," Hellman said casually.

Casker abruptly dropped the dust and wiped his hands.

"After all," Hellman pointed out, "granted that this is a warehouse—a cache, if you wish—we don't know what the late inhabitants considered good fare. Paris green salad, perhaps, with sulphuric acid as dressing."

"All right," Casker said, "but we gotta eat. What're you going to do about all this?" He gestured at the hundreds of boxes, cans and bottles.

"The thing to do," Hellman said briskly, "is to make a qualitative analysis on four or five samples. We could start out with a simple titration, sublimate the chief ingredient, see if it forms a precipitate, work out its molecular makeup from—"

"Hellman, you don't know what you're talking about. You're a librarian, remember? And I'm a correspondence school pilot. We don't know anything about titrations and sublimations."

"I know," Hellman said, "but we should. It's the right way to go about it."

"Sure. In the meantime, though, just until a chemist drops in, what'll we do?"

"This might help us," Hellman said, holding up the book. "Do you know what it is?"

"No," Casker said, keeping a tight grip on his patience.

"It's a pocket dictionary and guide to the Helg language."

"Helg?"

"The planet we're on. The symbols match up with those on the boxes."

Casker raised an eyebrow. "Never heard of Helg."

"I don't believe the planet has ever had any contact with Earth," Hellman said. "This dictionary isn't Helg-English. It's Helg-Aloombrigian."

Casker remembered that Aloombrigia was the home planet of a small, adventurous reptilian race, out near the center of the Galaxy.

"How come you can read Aloombrigian?" Casker asked.

"Oh, being a librarian isn't a completely useless profession," Hellman said modestly. "In my spare time—"

"Yeah. Now how about—"

"Do you know," Hellman said, "the Aloombrigians probably helped the Helgans leave their planet and find another. They sell services like that. In which case, this building very likely is a food cache!"

"Suppose you start translating," Casker suggested wearily, "and maybe find us something to eat."

They opened boxes until they found a likely-looking substance. Laboriously, Hellman translated the symbols on it.

"Got it," he said. "It reads:—'Use Sniffners—The Better Abrasive.'"

"Doesn't sound edible," Casker said.

"I'm afraid not."

They found another, which read: vigroom! fill all your stomachs, and fill them right!

"What kind of animals do you suppose these Helgans were?" Casker asked.

Hellman shrugged his shoulders.

The next label took almost fifteen minutes to translate. It read: argosel makes your thudra all tizzy. contains thirty arps of ramstat pulz, for shell lubrication.

"There must be something here we can eat," Casker said with a note of desperation.

"I hope so," Hellman replied.

At the end of two hours, they were no closer. They had translated dozens of titles and sniffed so many substances that their olfactory senses had given up in disgust.

"Let's talk this over," Hellman said, sitting on a box marked: vormitish—good as it sounds!

"Sure," Casker said, sprawling out on the floor. "Talk."

"If we could deduce what kind of creatures inhabited this planet, we'd know what kind of food they ate, and whether it's likely to be edible for us."

"All we do know is that they wrote a lot of lousy advertising copy."

Hellman ignored that. "What kind of intelligent beings would evolve on a planet that is all mountains?"

"Stupid ones!" Casker said.

That was no help. But Hellman found that he couldn't draw any inferences from the mountains. It didn't tell him if the late Helgans ate silicates or proteins or iodine-base foods or anything.

"Now look," Hellman said, "we'll have to work this out by pure logic— Are you listening to me?"

"Sure," Casker said.

"Okay. There's an old proverb that covers our situation perfectly: 'One man's meat is another man's poison.'"

"Yeah," Casker said. He was positive his stomach had shrunk to approximately the size of a marble.

"We can assume, first, that their meat is our meat."

Casker wrenched himself away from a vision of five juicy roast beefs dancing tantalizingly before him. "What if their meat is our poison? What then?"

"Then," Hellman said, "we will assume that their poison is our meat."

"And what happens if their meat and their poison are our poison?"

"We starve."

"All right," Casker said, standing up. "Which assumption do we start with?"

"Well, there's no sense in asking for trouble. This is an oxygen planet, if that means anything. Let's assume that we can eat some basic food of theirs. If we can't we'll start on their poisons."

"If we live that long," Casker said.

Hellman began to translate labels. They discarded such brands as androgynites' delight and verbell—for longer, curlier, more sensitive antennae, until they found a small gray box, about six inches by three by three. It was called valkorin's universal taste treat, for all digestive capacities.

"This looks as good as any," Hellman said. He opened the box.

Casker leaned over and sniffed. "No odor."

Within the box they found a rectangular, rubbery red block. It quivered slightly, like jelly.

"Bite into it," Casker said.

"Me?" Hellman asked. "Why not you?"

"You picked it."

"I prefer just looking at it," Hellman said with dignity. "I'm not too hungry."

"I'm not either," Casker said.

They sat on the floor and stared at the jellylike block. After ten minutes, Hellman yawned, leaned back and closed his eyes.

"All right, coward," Casker said bitterly. "I'll try it. Just remember, though, if I'm poisoned, you'll never get off this planet. You don't know how to pilot."

"Just take a little bite, then," Hellman advised.

Casker leaned over and stared at the block. Then he prodded it with his thumb.

The rubbery red block giggled.

"Did you hear that?" Casker yelped, leaping back.

"I didn't hear anything," Hellman said, his hands shaking. "Go ahead."

Casker prodded the block again. It giggled louder, this time with a disgusting little simper.

"Okay," Casker said, "what do we try next?"

"Next? What's wrong with this?"

"I don't eat anything that giggles," Casker stated firmly.

"Now listen to me," Hellman said. "The creatures who manufactured this might have been trying to create an esthetic sound as well as a pleasant shape and color. That giggle is probably only for the amusement of the eater."

"Then bite into it yourself," Casker offered.

Hellman glared at him, but made no move toward the rubbery block. Finally he said, "Let's move it out of the way."

They pushed the block over to a corner. It lay there giggling softly to itself.

"Now what?" Casker said.

Hellman looked around at the jumbled stacks of incomprehensible alien goods. He noticed a door on either side of the room.

"Let's have a look in the other sections," he suggested.

Casker shrugged his shoulders apathetically.

Slowly they trudged to the door in the left wall. It was locked and Hellman burned it open with the ship's burner.

It was a wedge-shaped room, piled with incomprehensible alien goods.

The hike back across the room seemed like miles, but they made it only slightly out of wind. Hellman blew out the lock and they looked in.

It was a wedge-shaped room, piled with incomprehensible alien goods.

"All the same," Casker said sadly, and closed the door.

"Evidently there's a series of these rooms going completely around the building," Hellman said. "I wonder if we should explore them."

Casker calculated the distance around the building, compared it with his remaining strength, and sat down heavily on a long gray object.

"Why bother?" he asked.

Hellman tried to collect his thoughts. Certainly he should be able to find a key of some sort, a clue that would tell him what they could eat. But where was it?

He examined the object Casker was sitting on. It was about the size and shape of a large coffin, with a shallow depression on top. It was made of a hard, corrugated substance.

"What do you suppose this is?" Hellman asked.

"Does it matter?"

Hellman glanced at the symbols painted on the side of the object, then looked them up in his dictionary.

"Fascinating," he murmured, after a while.

"Is it something to eat?" Casker asked, with a faint glimmering of hope.

"No, You are sitting on something called the morog custom super transport for the discriminating helgan who desires the best in vertical transportation. It's a vehicle!"

"Oh," Casker said dully.

"This is important! Look at it! How does it work?"

Casker wearily climbed off the Morog Custom Super Transport and looked it over carefully. He traced four almost invisible separations on its four corners. "Retractable wheels, probably, but I don't see—"

Hellman read on. "It says to give it three amphus of high-gain Integor fuel, then a van of Tonder lubrication, and not to run it over three thousand Ruls for the first fifty mungus."

"Let's find something to eat," Casker said.

"Don't you see how important this is?" Hellman asked. "This could solve our problem. If we could deduce the alien logic inherent in constructing this vehicle, we might know the Helgan thought pattern. This, in turn, would give us an insight into their nervous systems, which would imply their biochemical makeup."

Casker stood still, trying to decide whether he had enough strength left to strangle Hellman.

"For example," Hellman said, "what kind of vehicle would be used in a place like this? Not one with wheels, since everything is up and down. Anti-gravity? Perhaps, but what kind of anti-gravity? And why did the inhabitants devise a boxlike form instead—"

Casker decided sadly that he didn't have enough strength to strangle Hellman, no matter how pleasant it might be. Very quietly, he said, "Kindly stop making like a scientist. Let's see if there isn't something we can gulp down."

"All right," Hellman said sulkily.

Casker watched his partner wander off among the cans, bottles and cases. He wondered vaguely where Hellman got the energy, and decided that he was just too cerebral to know when he was starving.

"Here's something," Hellman called out, standing in front of a large yellow vat.

"What does it say?" Casker asked.

"Little bit hard to translate. But rendered freely, it reads: morishille's voozy, with lacto-ecto added for a new taste sensation. everyone drinks voozy. good before and after meals, no unpleasant after-effects. good for children! the drink of the universe!"

"That sounds good," Casker admitted, thinking that Hellman might not be so stupid after all.

"This should tell us once and for all if their meat is our meat," Hellman said. "This Voozy seems to be the closest thing to a universal drink I've found yet."

"Maybe," Casker said hopefully, "maybe it's just plain water!"

"We'll see." Hellman pried open the lid with the edge of the burner.

Within the vat was a crystal-clear liquid.

"No odor," Casker said, bending over the vat.

The crystal liquid lifted to meet him.

Casker retreated so rapidly that he fell over a box. Hellman helped him to his feet, and they approached the vat again. As they came near, the liquid lifted itself three feet into the air and moved toward them.

"What've you done now?" Casker asked, moving back carefully. The liquid flowed slowly over the side of the vat. It began to flow toward him.

"Hellman!" Casker shrieked.

Hellman was standing to one side, perspiration pouring down his face, reading his dictionary with a preoccupied frown.

"Guess I bumbled the translation," he said.

"Do something!" Casker shouted. The liquid was trying to back him into a corner.

"Nothing I can do," Hellman said, reading on. "Ah, here's the error. It doesn't say 'Everyone drinks Voozy.' Wrong subject. 'Voozy drinks everyone.' That tells us something! The Helgans must have soaked liquid in through their pores. Naturally, they would prefer to be drunk, instead of to drink."

Casker tried to dodge around the liquid, but it cut him off with a merry gurgle. Desperately he picked up a small bale and threw it at the Voozy. The Voozy caught the bale and drank it. Then it discarded that and turned back to Casker.

Hellman tossed another box. The Voozy drank this one and a third and fourth that Casker threw in. Then, apparently exhausted, it flowed back into its vat.

Casker clapped down the lid and sat on it, trembling violently.

"Not so good," Hellman said. "We've been taking it for granted that the Helgans had eating habits like us. But, of course, it doesn't necessarily—"

"No, it doesn't. No, sir, it certainly doesn't. I guess we can see that it doesn't. Anyone can see that it doesn't—"

"Stop that," Hellman ordered sternly. "We've no time for hysteria."

"Sorry." Casker slowly moved away from the Voozy vat.

"I guess we'll have to assume that their meat is our poison," Hellman said thoughtfully. "So now we'll see if their poison is our meat."

Casker didn't say anything. He was wondering what would have happened if the Voozy had drunk him.

In the corner, the rubbery block was still giggling to itself.

Now here's a likely-looking poison," Hellman said, half an hour later.

Casker had recovered completely, except for an occasional twitch of the lips.

"What does it say?" he asked.

Hellman rolled a tiny tube in the palm of his hand. "It's called Pvastkin's Plugger. The label reads: warning! highly dangerous! pvastkin's plugger is designed to fill holes or cracks of not more than two cubic vims. however—the plugger is not to be eaten under any circumstances. the active ingredient, ramotol, which makes pvastkin's so excellent a plugger renders it highly dangerous when taken internally."

"Sounds great," Casker said. "It'll probably blow us sky-high."

"Do you have any other suggestions?" Hellman asked.

Casker thought for a moment. The food of Helg was obviously unpalatable for humans. So perhaps was their poison ... but wasn't starvation better than this sort of thing?

After a moment's communion with his stomach, he decided that starvation was not better.

"Go ahead," he said.

Hellman slipped the burner under his arm and unscrewed the top of the little bottle. He shook it.

Nothing happened.

"It's got a seal," Casker pointed out.

Hellman punctured the seal with his fingernail and set the bottle on the floor. An evil-smelling green froth began to bubble out.

Hellman looked dubiously at the froth. It was congealing into a glob and spreading over the floor.

"Yeast, perhaps," he said, gripping the burner tightly.

"Come, come. Faint heart never filled an empty stomach."

"I'm not holding you back," Hellman said.

The glob swelled to the size of a man's head.

"How long is that supposed to go on?" Casker asked.

"Well," Hellman said, "it's advertised as a Plugger. I suppose that's what it does—expands to plug up holes."

"Sure. But how much?"

"Unfortunately, I don't know how much two cubic vims are. But it can't go on much—"

Belatedly, they noticed that the Plugger had filled almost a quarter of the room and was showing no signs of stopping.

"We should have believed the label!" Casker yelled to him, across the spreading glob. "It is dangerous!"

As the Plugger produced more surface, it began to accelerate in its growth. A sticky edge touched Hellman, and he jumped back.

"Watch out!"

He couldn't reach Casker, on the other side of the gigantic sphere of blob. Hellman tried to run around, but the Plugger had spread, cutting the room in half. It began to swell toward the walls.

"Run for it!" Hellman yelled, and rushed to the door behind him.

He flung it open just as the expanding glob reached him. On the other side of the room, he heard a door slam shut. Hellman didn't wait any longer. He sprinted through and slammed the door behind him.

He stood for a moment, panting, the burner in his hand. He hadn't realized how weak he was. That sprint had cut his reserves of energy dangerously close to the collapsing point. At least Casker had made it, too, though.

But he was still in trouble.

The Plugger poured merrily through the blasted lock, into the room. Hellman tried a practice shot on it, but the Plugger was evidently impervious ... as, he realized, a good plugger should be.

It was showing no signs of fatigue.

Hellman hurried to the far wall. The door was locked, as the others had been, so he burned out the lock and went through.

How far could the glob expand? How much was two cubic vims? Two cubic miles, perhaps? For all he knew, the Plugger was used to repair faults in the crusts of planets.

In the next room, Hellman stopped to catch his breath. He remembered that the building was circular. He would burn his way through the remaining doors and join Casker. They would burn their way outside and....

Casker didn't have a burner!

Hellman turned white with shock. Casker had made it into the room on the right, because they had burned it open earlier. The Plugger was undoubtedly oozing into that room, through the shattered lock ... and Casker couldn't get out! The Plugger was on his left, a locked door on his right!

Rallying his remaining strength, Hellman began to run. Boxes seemed to get in his way purposefully, tripping him, slowing him down. He blasted the next door and hurried on to the next. And the next. And the next.

The Plugger couldn't expand completely into Casker's room!

Or could it?

The wedge-shaped rooms, each a segment of a circle, seemed to stretch before him forever, a jumbled montage of locked doors, alien goods, more doors, more goods. Hellman fell over a crate, got to his feet and fell again. He had reached the limit of his strength, and passed it. But Casker was his friend.

Besides, without a pilot, he'd never get off the place.

Hellman struggled through two more rooms on trembling legs and then collapsed in front of a third.

"Is that you, Hellman?" he heard Casker ask, from the other side of the door.

"You all right?" Hellman managed to gasp.

"Haven't much room in here," Casker said, "but the Plugger's stopped growing. Hellman, get me out of here!"

Hellman lay on the floor panting. "Moment," he said.

"Moment, hell!" Casker shouted. "Get me out. I've found water!"

"What? How?"

"Get me out of here!"

Hellman tried to stand up, but his legs weren't cooperating. "What happened?" he asked.

"When I saw that glob filling the room, I figured I'd try to start up the Super Custom Transport. Thought maybe it could knock down the door and get me out. So I pumped it full of high-gain Integor fuel."

"Yes?" Hellman said, still trying to get his legs under control.

"That Super Custom Transport is an animal, Hellman! And the Integor fuel is water! Now get me out!"

Hellman lay back with a contented sigh. If he had had a little more time, he would have worked out the whole thing himself, by pure logic. But it was all very apparent now. The most efficient machine to go over those vertical, razor-sharp mountains would be an animal, probably with retractable suckers. It was kept in hibernation between trips; and if it drank water, the other products designed for it would be palatable, too. Of course they still didn't know much about the late inhabitants, but undoubtedly....

"Burn down that door!" Casker shrieked, his voice breaking.

Hellman was pondering the irony of it all. If one man's meat—and his poison—are your poison, then try eating something else. So simple, really.

But there was one thing that still bothered him.

"How did you know it was an Earth-type animal?" he asked.

"Its breath, stupid! It inhales and exhales and smells as if it's eaten onions!" There was a sound of cans falling and bottles shattering. "Now hurry!"

"What's wrong?" Hellman asked, finally getting to his feet and poising the burner.

"The Custom Super Transport. It's got me cornered behind a pile of cases. Hellman, it seems to think that I'm its meat!"

Broiled with the burner—well done for Hellman, medium rare for Casker—it was their meat, with enough left over for the trip back to Calao.

—ROBERT SHECKLEY

Warm

Illustrated by EMSH

It was a joyous journey Anders set out on ... to reach his goal ... but look where he wound up!

Anders lay on his bed, fully dressed except for his shoes and black bow tie, contemplating, with a certain uneasiness, the evening before him. In twenty minutes he would pick up Judy at her apartment, and that was the uneasy part of it.

He had realized, only seconds ago, that he was in love with her.

Well, he'd tell her. The evening would be memorable. He would propose, there would be kisses, and the seal of acceptance would, figuratively speaking, be stamped across his forehead.

Not too pleasant an outlook, he decided. It really would be much more comfortable not to be in love. What had done it? A look, a touch, a thought? It didn't take much, he knew, and stretched his arms for a thorough yawn.

"Help me!" a voice said.

His muscles spasmed, cutting off the yawn in mid-moment. He sat upright on the bed, then grinned and lay back again.

"You must help me!" the voice insisted.

Anders sat up, reached for a polished shoe and fitted it on, giving his full attention to the tying of the laces.

"Can you hear me?" the voice asked. "You can, can't you?"

That did it. "Yes, I can hear you," Anders said, still in a high good humor. "Don't tell me you're my guilty subconscious, attacking me for a childhood trauma I never bothered to resolve. I suppose you want me to join a monastery."

"I don't know what you're talking about," the voice said. "I'm no one's subconscious. I'm me. Will you help me?"

Anders believed in voices as much as anyone; that is, he didn't believe in them at all, until he heard them. Swiftly he catalogued the possibilities. Schizophrenia was the best answer, of course, and one in which his colleagues would concur. But Anders had a lamentable confidence in his own sanity. In which case—

"Who are you?" he asked.

"I don't know," the voice answered.

Anders realized that the voice was speaking within his own mind. Very suspicious.

"You don't know who you are," Anders stated. "Very well. Where are you?"

"I don't know that, either." The voice paused, and went on. "Look, I know how ridiculous this must sound. Believe me, I'm in some sort of limbo. I don't know how I got here or who I am, but I want desperately to get out. Will you help me?"

Still fighting the idea of a voice speaking within his head, Anders knew that his next decision was vital. He had to accept—or reject—his own sanity.

He accepted it.

"All right," Anders said, lacing the other shoe. "I'll grant that you're a person in trouble, and that you're in some sort of telepathic contact with me. Is there anything else you can tell me?"

"I'm afraid not," the voice said, with infinite sadness. "You'll have to find out for yourself."

"Can you contact anyone else?"

"No."

"Then how can you talk with me?"

"I don't know."

Anders walked to his bureau mirror and adjusted his black bow tie, whistling softly under his breath. Having just discovered that he was in love, he wasn't going to let a little thing like a voice in his mind disturb him.

"I really don't see how I can be of any help," Anders said, brushing a bit of lint from his jacket. "You don't know where you are, and there don't seem to be any distinguishing landmarks. How am I to find you?" He turned and looked around the room to see if he had forgotten anything.

"I'll know when you're close," the voice said. "You were warm just then."

"Just then?" All he had done was look around the room. He did so again, turning his head slowly. Then it happened.

The room, from one angle, looked different. It was suddenly a mixture of muddled colors, instead of the carefully blended pastel shades he had selected. The lines of wall, floor and ceiling were strangely off proportion, zigzag, unrelated.

Then everything went back to normal.

"You were very warm," the voice said. "It's a question of seeing things correctly."

Anders resisted the urge to scratch his head, for fear of disarranging his carefully combed hair. What he had seen wasn't so strange. Everyone sees one or two things in his life that make him doubt his normality, doubt sanity, doubt his very existence. For a moment the orderly Universe is disarranged and the fabric of belief is ripped.

But the moment passes.

Anders remembered once, as a boy, awakening in his room in the middle of the night. How strange everything had looked. Chairs, table, all out of proportion, swollen in the dark. The ceiling pressing down, as in a dream.

But that had also passed.

"Well, old man," he said, "if I get warm again, let me know."

"I will," the voice in his head whispered. "I'm sure you'll find me."

"I'm glad you're so sure," Anders said gaily, switched off the lights and left.

Lovely and smiling, Judy greeted him at the door. Looking at her, Anders sensed her knowledge of the moment. Had she felt the change in him, or predicted it? Or was love making him grin like an idiot?

"Would you like a before-party drink?" she asked.

He nodded, and she led him across the room, to the improbable green-and-yellow couch. Sitting down, Anders decided he would tell her when she came back with the drink. No use in putting off the fatal moment. A lemming in love, he told himself.

"You're getting warm again," the voice said.

He had almost forgotten his invisible friend. Or fiend, as the case could well be. What would Judy say if she knew he was hearing voices? Little things like that, he reminded himself, often break up the best of romances.

"Here," she said, handing him a drink.

Still smiling, he noticed. The number two smile—to a prospective suitor, provocative and understanding. It had been preceded, in their relationship, by the number one nice-girl smile, the don't-misunderstand-me smile, to be worn on all occasions, until the correct words have been mumbled.

"That's right," the voice said. "It's in how you look at things."

Look at what? Anders glanced at Judy, annoyed at his thoughts. If he was going to play the lover, let him play it. Even through the astigmatic haze of love, he was able to appreciate her blue-gray eyes, her fine skin (if one overlooked a tiny blemish on the left temple), her lips, slightly reshaped by lipstick.

"How did your classes go today?" she asked.

Well, of course she'd ask that, Anders thought. Love is marking time.

"All right," he said. "Teaching psychology to young apes—"

"Oh, come now!"

"Warmer," the voice said.

What's the matter with me, Anders wondered. She really is a lovely girl. The gestalt that is Judy, a pattern of thoughts, expressions, movements, making up the girl I—

I what?

Love?

Anders shifted his long body uncertainly on the couch. He didn't quite understand how this train of thought had begun. It annoyed him. The analytical young instructor was better off in the classroom. Couldn't science wait until 9:10 in the morning?

"I was thinking about you today," Judy said, and Anders knew that she had sensed the change in his mood.

"Do you see?" the voice asked him. "You're getting much better at it."

"I don't see anything," Anders thought, but the voice was right. It was as though he had a clear line of inspection into Judy's mind. Her feelings were nakedly apparent to him, as meaningless as his room had been in that flash of undistorted thought.

"I really was thinking about you," she repeated.

"Now look," the voice said.

Anders, watching the expressions on Judy's face, felt the strangeness descend on him. He was back in the nightmare perception of that moment in his room. This time it was as though he were watching a machine in a laboratory. The object of this operation was the evocation and preservation of a particular mood. The machine goes through a searching process, invoking trains of ideas to achieve the desired end.

"Oh, were you?" he asked, amazed at his new perspective.

"Yes ... I wondered what you were doing at noon," the reactive machine opposite him on the couch said, expanding its shapely chest slightly.

"Good," the voice said, commending him for his perception.

"Dreaming of you, of course," he said to the flesh-clad skeleton behind the total gestalt Judy. The flesh machine rearranged its limbs, widened its mouth to denote pleasure. The mechanism searched through a complex of fears, hopes, worries, through half-remembrances of analogous situations, analogous solutions.

And this was what he loved. Anders saw too clearly and hated himself for seeing. Through his new nightmare perception, the absurdity of the entire room struck him.

"Were you really?" the articulating skeleton asked him.

"You're coming closer," the voice whispered.

To what? The personality? There was no such thing. There was no true cohesion, no depth, nothing except a web of surface reactions, stretched across automatic visceral movements.

He was coming closer to the truth.

"Sure," he said sourly.

The machine stirred, searching for a response.

Anders felt a quick tremor of fear at the sheer alien quality of his viewpoint. His sense of formalism had been sloughed off, his agreed-upon reactions bypassed. What would be revealed next?

He was seeing clearly, he realized, as perhaps no man had ever seen before. It was an oddly exhilarating thought.

But could he still return to normality?

"Can I get you a drink?" the reaction machine asked.

At that moment Anders was as thoroughly out of love as a man could be. Viewing one's intended as a depersonalized, sexless piece of machinery is not especially conducive to love. But it is quite stimulating, intellectually.

Anders didn't want normality. A curtain was being raised and he wanted to see behind it. What was it some Russian scientist—Ouspensky, wasn't it—had said?

"Think in other categories."

That was what he was doing, and would continue to do.

"Good-by," he said suddenly.

The machine watched him, open-mouthed, as he walked out the door. Delayed circuit reactions kept it silent until it heard the elevator door close.

"You were very warm in there," the voice within his head whispered, once he was on the street. "But you still don't understand everything."

"Tell me, then," Anders said, marveling a little at his equanimity. In an hour he had bridged the gap to a completely different viewpoint, yet it seemed perfectly natural.

"I can't," the voice said. "You must find it yourself."

"Well, let's see now," Anders began. He looked around at the masses of masonry, the convention of streets cutting through the architectural piles. "Human life," he said, "is a series of conventions. When you look at a girl, you're supposed to see—a pattern, not the underlying formlessness."

"That's true," the voice agreed, but with a shade of doubt.

"Basically, there is no form. Man produces gestalts, and cuts form out of the plethora of nothingness. It's like looking at a set of lines and saying that they represent a figure. We look at a mass of material, extract it from the background and say it's a man. But in truth there is no such thing. There are only the humanizing features that we—myopically—attach to it. Matter is conjoined, a matter of viewpoint."

"You're not seeing it now," said the voice.

"Damn it," Anders said. He was certain that he was on the track of something big, perhaps something ultimate. "Everyone's had the experience. At some time in his life, everyone looks at a familiar object and can't make any sense out of it. Momentarily, the gestalt fails, but the true moment of sight passes. The mind reverts to the superimposed pattern. Normalcy continues."

The voice was silent. Anders walked on, through the gestalt city.

"There's something else, isn't there?" Anders asked.

"Yes."

What could that be, he asked himself. Through clearing eyes, Anders looked at the formality he had called his world.

He wondered momentarily if he would have come to this if the voice hadn't guided him. Yes, he decided after a few moments, it was inevitable.

But who was the voice? And what had he left out?

"Let's see what a party looks like now," he said to the voice.

The party was a masquerade; the guests were all wearing their faces.

To Anders, their motives, individually and collectively, were painfully apparent. Then his vision began to clear further.

He saw that the people weren't truly individual. They were discontinuous lumps of flesh sharing a common vocabulary, yet not even truly discontinuous.

The lumps of flesh were a part of the decoration of the room and almost indistinguishable from it. They were one with the lights, which lent their tiny vision. They were joined to the sounds they made, a few feeble tones out of the great possibility of sound. They blended into the walls.

The kaleidoscopic view came so fast that Anders had trouble sorting his new impressions. He knew now that these people existed only as patterns, on the same basis as the sounds they made and the things they thought they saw.

Gestalts, sifted out of the vast, unbearable real world.

"Where's Judy?" a discontinuous lump of flesh asked him. This particular lump possessed enough nervous mannerisms to convince the other lumps of his reality. He wore a loud tie as further evidence.

"She's sick," Anders said. The flesh quivered into an instant sympathy. Lines of formal mirth shifted to formal woe.

"Hope it isn't anything serious," the vocal flesh remarked.

"You're warmer," the voice said to Anders.

Anders looked at the object in front of him.

"She hasn't long to live," he stated.

The flesh quivered. Stomach and intestines contracted in sympathetic fear. Eyes distended, mouth quivered.

The loud tie remained the same.

"My God! You don't mean it!"

"What are you?" Anders asked quietly.

"What do you mean?" the indignant flesh attached to the tie demanded. Serene within its reality, it gaped at Anders. Its mouth twitched, undeniable proof that it was real and sufficient. "You're drunk," it sneered.

Anders laughed and left the party.

"There is still something you don't know," the voice said. "But you were hot! I could feel you near me."

"What are you?" Anders asked again.

"I don't know," the voice admitted. "I am a person. I am I. I am trapped."

"So are we all," Anders said. He walked on asphalt, surrounded by heaps of concrete, silicates, aluminum and iron alloys. Shapeless, meaningless heaps that made up the gestalt city.

And then there were the imaginary lines of demarcation dividing city from city, the artificial boundaries of water and land.

All ridiculous.

"Give me a dime for some coffee, mister?" something asked, a thing indistinguishable from any other thing.

"Old Bishop Berkeley would give a nonexistent dime to your nonexistent presence," Anders said gaily.

"I'm really in a bad way," the voice whined, and Anders perceived that it was no more than a series of modulated vibrations.

"Yes! Go on!" the voice commanded.

"If you could spare me a quarter—" the vibrations said, with a deep pretense at meaning.

No, what was there behind the senseless patterns? Flesh, mass. What was that? All made up of atoms.

"I'm really hungry," the intricately arranged atoms muttered.

All atoms. Conjoined. There were no true separations between atom and atom. Flesh was stone, stone was light. Anders looked at the masses of atoms that were pretending to solidity, meaning and reason.

"Can't you help me?" a clump of atoms asked. But the clump was identical with all the other atoms. Once you ignored the superimposed patterns, you could see the atoms were random, scattered.

"I don't believe in you," Anders said.

The pile of atoms was gone.

"Yes!" the voice cried. "Yes!"

"I don't believe in any of it," Anders said. After all, what was an atom?

"Go on!" the voice shouted. "You're hot! Go on!"

What was an atom? An empty space surrounded by an empty space. Absurd!

"Then it's all false!" Anders said. And he was alone under the stars.

"That's right!" the voice within his head screamed. "Nothing!"

But stars, Anders thought. How can one believe—

The stars disappeared. Anders was in a gray nothingness, a void. There was nothing around him except shapeless gray.

Where was the voice?

Gone.

Anders perceived the delusion behind the grayness, and then there was nothing at all.

Complete nothingness, and himself within it.

Where was he? What did it mean? Anders' mind tried to add it up.

Impossible. *That* couldn't be true.

Again the score was tabulated, but Anders' mind couldn't accept the total. In desperation, the overloaded mind erased the figures, eradicated the knowledge, erased itself.

"Where am I?"

In nothingness. Alone.

Trapped.

"Who am I?"

A voice.

The voice of Anders searched the nothingness, shouted, "Is there anyone here?"

No answer.

But there was someone. All directions were the same, yet moving along one he could make contact ... with someone. The voice of Anders reached back to someone who could save him, perhaps.

"Save me," the voice said to Anders, lying fully dressed on his bed, except for his shoes and black bow tie.

KEEP YOUR SHAPE

Illustrated by VIDMER

Only a race as incredibly elastic as the Grom could have a single rule of war:

Pid the Pilot slowed the ship almost to a standstill, and peered anxiously at the green planet below.

Even without instruments, there was no mistaking it. Third from its sun, it was the only planet in this system capable of sustaining life. Peacefully it swam beneath its gauze of clouds.

It looked very innocent. And yet, twenty previous Grom expeditions had set out to prepare this planet for invasion—and vanished utterly, without a word.

Pid hesitated only a moment, before starting irrevocably down. There was no point in hovering and worrying. He and his two crewmen were as ready now as they would ever be. Their compact Displacers were stored in body pouches, inactive but ready.

Pid wanted to say something to his crew, but wasn't sure how to put it.

The crew waited. Ilg the Radioman had sent the final message to the Grom planet. Ger the Detector read sixteen dials at once, and reported, "No sign of alien activity." His body surfaces flowed carelessly.

Noticing the flow, Pid knew what to say to his crew. Ever since they had left Grom, shape-discipline had been disgustingly lax. The Invasion Chief had warned him; but still, he had to do something about it. It was his duty, since lower castes such as Radiomen and Detectors were notoriously prone to Shapelessness.

"A lot of hopes are resting on this expedition," he began slowly. "We're a long way from home now."

Ger the Detector nodded. Ilg the Radioman flowed out of his prescribed shape and molded himself comfortably to a wall.

"However," Pid said sternly, "distance is no excuse for promiscuous Shapelessness."

Ilg flowed hastily back into proper Radioman's shape.

"Exotic forms will undoubtedly be called for," Pid went on. "And for that we have a special dispensation. But remember—any shape not assumed strictly in the line of duty is a foul, lawless device of The Shapeless One!"

Ger's body surfaces abruptly stopped flowing.

"That's all," Pid said, and flowed into his controls. The ship started down, so smoothly coordinated that Pid felt a glow of pride.

They were good workers, he decided. He just couldn't expect them to be as shape-conscious as a high-caste Pilot. Even the Invasion Chief had told him that.

"Pid," the Invasion Chief had said at their last interview, "we need this planet desperately."

"Yes, sir," Pid had said, standing at full attention, never quivering from Optimum Pilot's Shape.

"One of you," the Chief said heavily, "must get through and set up a Displacer near an atomic power source. The army will be standing by at this end, ready to step through."

"We'll do it, sir," Pid said.

"This expedition has to succeed," the Chief said, and his features blurred momentarily from sheer fatigue. "In strictest confidence, there's considerable unrest on Grom. The Miner caste is on strike, for instance. They want a new digging shape. Say the old one is inefficient."

Pid looked properly indignant. The Mining Shape had been set down by the Ancients fifty thousand years ago, together with the rest of the basic shapes. And now these upstarts wanted to change it!

"That's not all," the Chief told him. "We've uncovered a new Cult of Shapelessness. Picked up almost eight thousand Grom, and I don't know how many more we missed."

Pid knew that Shapelessness was a lure of The Shapeless One, the greatest evil that the Grom mind could conceive of. But why, he wondered, did so many

Grom fall for His lures?

The Chief guessed his question. "Pid," he said, "I suppose it's difficult
for you to understand. Do you enjoy Piloting?"

"Yes, sir," Pid said simply. Enjoy Piloting! It was his entire life! Without
a ship, he was nothing.

"Not all Grom feel that way," the Chief said. "I don't understand it either. All my ancestors have been Invasion Chiefs, back to the beginning
of time. So of course I want to be an Invasion Chief. It's only natural, as
well as lawful. But the lower castes don't feel that way." The Chief shook
his body sadly. "I've told you this for a reason. We Grom need more room.
This unrest is caused purely by crowding. All our psychologists say so.
Another planet to expand into will cure everything. So we're counting on
you, Pid."

"Yes, sir," Pid said, with a glow of pride.

The Chief rose to end the interview. Then he changed his mind and sat
down again.

"You'll have to watch your crew," he said. "They're loyal, no doubt, but
low-caste. And you know the lower castes."

Pid did indeed.

"Ger, your Detector, is suspected of harboring Alterationist tendencies.
He was once fined for assuming a quasi-Hunter shape. Ilg has never had
any definite charge brought against him. But I hear that he remains im-
mobile for suspiciously long periods of time. Possibly, he fancies himself
a Thinker."

"But, sir," Pid protested. "If they are even slightly tainted with Altera-
tionism or Shapelessness, why send them on this expedition?"

The Chief hesitated before answering. "There are plenty of Grom I could
trust," he said slowly. "But those two have certain qualities of resourcefulness and imagination that will be needed on this expedition." He
sighed. "I really don't understand why those qualities are usually linked
with Shapelessness."

"Yes, sir," Pid said.

"Just watch them."

"Yes, sir," Pid said again, and saluted, realizing that the interview was
at an end. In his body pouch he felt the dormant Displacer, ready to
transform the enemy's power source into a bridge across space for the
Grom hordes.

"Good luck," the chief said. "I'm sure you'll need it."

The ship dropped silently toward the surface of the enemy planet. Ger
the Detector analyzed the clouds below, and fed data into the Camouflage Unit. The Unit went to work. Soon the ship looked, to all outward
appearances, like a cirrus formation.

Pid allowed the ship to drift slowly toward the surface of the mystery planet. He was in Optimum Pilot's Shape now, the most efficient of the four shapes allotted to the Pilot caste. Blind, deaf and dumb, an extension of his controls, all his attention was directed toward matching the velocities of the high-flying clouds, staying among them, becoming a part of them.

Ger remained rigidly in one of the two shapes allotted to Detectors. He fed data into the Camouflage Unit, and the descending ship slowly altered into an alto-cumulus.

There was no sign of activity from the enemy planet.

Ilg located an atomic power source, and fed the data to Pid. The Pilot altered course. He had reached the lowest level of clouds, barely a mile above the surface of the planet. Now his ship looked like a fat, fleecy cumulus.

And still there was no sign of alarm. The unknown fate that had overtaken twenty previous expeditions still had not showed itself.

Dusk crept across the face of the planet as Pid maneuvered near the atomic power installation. He avoided the surrounding homes and hovered over a clump of woods.

Darkness fell, and the green planet's lone moon was veiled in clouds.

One cloud floated lower.

And landed.

"Quick, everyone out!" Pid shouted, detaching himself from the ship's controls. He assumed the Pilot's Shape best suited for running, and raced out the hatch. Ger and Ilg hurried after him. They stopped fifty yards from the ship, and waited.

Inside the ship a little-used circuit closed. There was a silent shudder, and the ship began to melt. Plastic dissolved, metal crumpled. Soon the ship was a great pile of junk, and still the process went on. Big fragments broke into smaller fragments, and split, and split again.

Pid felt suddenly helpless, watching his ship scuttle itself. He was a Pilot, of the Pilot caste. His father had been a Pilot, and his father before him, stretching back to the hazy past when the Grom had first constructed ships. He had spent his entire childhood around ships, his entire manhood flying them.

Now, shipless, he was naked in an alien world.

In a few minutes there was only a mound of dust to show where the ship had been. The night wind scattered it through the forest. And then there was nothing at all.

They waited. Nothing happened. The wind sighed and the trees creaked. Squirrels chirped, and birds stirred in their nests. An acorn fell to the ground.

Pid heaved a sigh of relief and sat down. The twenty-first Grom expedition had landed safely.

There was nothing to be done until morning, so Pid began to make plans. They had landed as close to the atomic power installation as they dared. Now they would have to get closer. Somehow, one of them had to get very near the reactor room, in order to activate the Displacer.

Difficult. But Pid felt certain of success. After all, the Grom were strong on ingenuity.

Strong on ingenuity, he thought bitterly, but terribly short of radioactives. That was another reason why this expedition was so important. There was little radioactive fuel left, on any of the Grom worlds. Ages ago, the Grom had spent their store of radioactives in spreading throughout their neighboring worlds, occupying the ones that they could live on.

Now, colonization barely kept up with the mounting birthrate. New worlds were constantly needed.

This particular world, discovered in a scouting expedition, was needed. It suited the Grom perfectly. But it was too far away. They didn't have enough fuel to mount a conquering space fleet.

Luckily, there was another way. A better way.

Over the centuries, the Grom scientists had developed the Displacer. A triumph of Identity Engineering, the Displacer allowed mass to be moved instantaneously between any two linked points.

One end was set up at Grom's sole atomic energy plant. The other end had to be placed in proximity to another atomic power source, and activated. Diverted power then flowed through both ends, was modified, and modified again.

Then, through the miracle of Identity Engineering, the Grom could step through from planet to planet; or pour through in a great, overwhelming wave.

It was quite simple.

But twenty expeditions had failed to set up the Earth-end Displacer.

What had happened to them was not known.

For no Grom ship had ever returned to tell.

Before dawn they crept through the woods, taking on the coloration of the plants around them. Their Displacers pulsed feebly, sensing the nearness of atomic energy.

A tiny, four-legged creature darted in front of them. Instantly, Ger grew four legs and a long, streamlined body and gave chase.

"Ger! Come back here!" Pid howled at the Detector, throwing caution to the winds.

Ger overtook the animal and knocked it down. He tried to bite it, but he had neglected to grow teeth. The animal jumped free, and vanished into the underbrush. Ger thrust out a set of teeth and bunched his muscles for another leap.

"Ger!"

Reluctantly, the Detector turned away. He loped silently back to Pid.

"I was hungry," he said.

"You were not," Pid said sternly.

"Was," Ger mumbled, writhing with embarrassment.

Pid remembered what the Chief had told him. Ger certainly did have Hunter tendencies. He would have to watch him more closely.

"We'll have no more of that," Pid said. "Remember—the lure of Exotic Shapes is not sanctioned. Be content with the shape you were born to."

Ger nodded, and melted back into the underbrush. They moved on.

At the extreme edge of the woods they could observe the atomic energy installation. Pid disguised himself as a clump of shrubbery, and Ger formed himself into an old log. Ilg, after a moment's thought, became a young oak.

The installation was in the form of a long, low building, surrounded by a metal fence. There was a gate, and guards in front of it.

The first job, Pid thought, was to get past that gate. He began to consider ways and means.

From the fragmentary reports of the survey parties, Pid knew that, in some ways, this race of Men were like the Grom. They had pets, as the Grom did, and homes and children, and a culture. The inhabitants were skilled mechanically, as were the Grom.

But there were terrific differences, also. The Men were of fixed and immutable form, like stones or trees. And to compensate, their planet boasted a fantastic array of species, types and kinds. This was completely unlike Grom, which had only eight distinct forms of animal life.

And evidently, the Men were skilled at detecting invaders, Pid thought. He wished he knew how the other expeditions had failed. It would make his job much easier.

A Man lurched past them on two incredibly stiff legs. Rigidity was evident in his every move. Without looking, he hurried past.

"I know," Ger said, after the creature had moved away. "I'll disguise myself as a Man, walk through the gate to the reactor room, and activate my Displacer."

"You can't speak their language," Pid pointed out.

"I won't speak at all. I'll ignore them. Look." Quickly Ger shaped himself into a Man.

"That's not bad," Pid said.

Ger tried a few practice steps, copying the bumpy walk of the Man.

"But I'm afraid it won't work," Pid said.

"It's perfectly logical," Ger pointed out.

"I know. Therefore the other expeditions must have tried it. And none of them came back."

There was no arguing that. Ger flowed back into the shape of a log. "What, then?" he asked.

"Let me think," Pid said.

Another creature lurched past, on four legs instead of two. Pid recognized it as a Dog, a pet of Man. He watched it carefully.

The Dog ambled to the gate, head down, in no particular hurry. It walked through, unchallenged, and lay down in the grass.

"H'm," Pid said.

They watched. One of the Men walked past, and touched the Dog on the head. The Dog stuck out its tongue and rolled over on its side.

"I can do that," Ger said excitedly. He started to flow into the shape of a Dog.

"No, wait," Pid said. "We'll spend the rest of the day thinking it over. This is too important to rush into."

Ger subsided sulkily.

"Come on, let's move back," Pid said. He and Ger started into the woods. Then he remembered Ilg.

"Ilg?" he called softly.

There was no answer.

"Ilg!"

"What? Oh, yes," an oak tree said, and melted into a bush. "Sorry. What were you saying?"

"We're moving back," Pid said. "Were you, by any chance, Thinking?"

"Oh, no," Ilg assured him. "Just resting."

Pid let it go at that. There was too much else to worry about.

They discussed it for the rest of the day, hidden in the deepest part of the woods. The only alternatives seemed to be Man or Dog. A Tree couldn't walk past the gates, since that was not in the nature of trees. Nor could anything else, and escape notice.

Going as a Man seemed too risky. They decided that Ger would sally out in the morning as a Dog.

"Now get some sleep," Pid said.

Obediently his two crewmen flattened out, going immediately Shapeless. But Pid had a more difficult time.

Everything looked too easy. Why wasn't the atomic installation better guarded? Certainly the Men must have learned something from the expeditions they had captured in the past. Or had they killed them without asking any questions?

You couldn't tell what an alien would do.

Was that open gate a trap?

Wearily he flowed into a comfortable position on the lumpy ground. Then he pulled himself together hastily.

He had gone Shapeless!

Comfort was not in the line of duty, he reminded himself, and firmly took a Pilot's Shape.

But a Pilot's Shape wasn't constructed for sleeping on damp, bumpy ground. Pid spent a restless night, thinking of ships, and wishing he were flying one.

He awoke in the morning tired and ill-tempered. He nudged Ger.

"Let's get this over with," he said.

Ger flowed gaily to his feet.

"Come on, Ilg," Pid said angrily, looking around. "Wake up."

There was no reply.

"Ilg!" he called.

Still there was no reply.

"Help me look for him," Pid said to Ger. "He must be around here somewhere."

Together they tested every bush, tree, log and shrub in the vicinity. But none of them was Ilg.

Pid began to feel a cold panic run through him. What could have happened to the Radioman?

"Perhaps he decided to go through the gate on his own," Ilg suggested.

Pid considered the possibility. It seemed unlikely. Ilg had never shown much initiative. He had always been content to follow orders.

They waited. But midday came, and there was still no sign of Ilg.

"We can't wait any longer," Pid said, and they started through the woods. Pid wondered if Ilg had tried to get through the gates on his own. Those quiet types often concealed a foolhardy streak.

But there was nothing to show that Ilg had been successful. He would have to assume that the Radioman was dead, or captured by the Men.

That left two of them to activate a Displacer.

And he *still* didn't know what had happened to the other expeditions.

At the edge of the woods, Ger turned himself into a facsimile of a Dog. Pid inspected him carefully.

"A little less tail," he said.

Ger shortened his tail.

"More ears."

Ger lengthened his ears,

"Now even them up."

They became even.

Pid inspected the finished product. As far as he could tell, Ger was perfect, from the tip of his tail to his wet, black nose.

"Good luck," Pid said.

"Thanks." Cautiously Ger moved out of the woods, walking in the lurching style of Dogs and Men. At the gate the guard called to him. Pid held his breath.

Ger walked past the Man, ignoring him. The Man started to walk over. Ger broke into a run.

Pid shaped a pair of strong legs for himself, ready to dash if Ger was caught.

But the guard turned back to his gate. Ger stopped running immediately, and strolled quietly toward the main door of the building.

Pid dissolved his legs with a sigh of relief ... and then tensed again.

The main door was closed!

Pid hoped the Radioman wouldn't try to open it. That was not in the nature of Dogs.

As he watched, another Dog came running toward Ger. Ger backed away from him. The Dog approached and sniffed. Ger sniffed back.

Then both of them ran around the building.

That was clever, Pid thought. There was bound to be a door in the rear.

He glanced up at the afternoon sun. As soon as the Displacer was activated, the Grom armies would begin to pour through. By the time the Men recovered from the shock, a million or more Grom troops would be here, weapons and all. With more following.

The day passed slowly, and nothing happened.

Nervously Pid watched the front of the plant. It shouldn't be taking so long, if Ger were successful.

Late into the night he waited. Men walked in and out of the installation, and Dogs barked around the gates. But Ger did not appear.

Ger had failed. Ilg was gone. Only he was left.

And still he didn't know what had happened.

By morning, Pid was in complete despair. He knew that the twenty-first Grom expedition to this planet was near the point of complete failure. Now it was all up to him.

He saw that workers were arriving in great number, rushing through the gates. He decided to take advantage of the apparent confusion, and started to shape himself into a Man.

A Dog walked past the woods where he was hiding.

"Hello," the Dog said.

It was Ger!

"What happened?" Pid asked, with a sigh of relief. "Why were you so long? Couldn't you get in?"

"I don't know," Ger said, wagging his tail. "I didn't try."

Pid was speechless.

"I went hunting," Ger said complacently. "This form is ideal for Hunting, you know. I went out the rear gate with another Dog."

"But the expedition—your duty—"

"I changed my mind," Ger told him. "You know, Pilot, I never wanted to be a Detector."

"But you were *born* a Detector!"

"That's true," Ger said. "But it doesn't help. I always wanted to be a Hunter."

Pid shook his entire body in annoyance. "You can't," he said, very slowly, as one would explain to a Gromling. "The Hunter shape is forbidden to you."

"Not here it isn't," Ger said, still wagging his tail.

"Let's have no more of this," Pid said angrily. "Get into that installation and set up your Displacer. I'll try to overlook this heresy."

"No," Ger said. "I don't want the Grom here. They'd ruin it for the rest of us."

"He's right," a nearby oak tree said.

"Ilg!" Pid gasped. "Where are you?"

Branches stirred. "I'm right here," Ilg said. "I've been Thinking."

"But—your caste—"

"Pilot," Ger said sadly, "why don't you wake up? Most of the people on Grom are miserable. Only custom makes us take the caste-shape of our ancestors."

"Pilot," Ilg said, "all Grom are born Shapeless!"

"And being born Shapeless, all Grom should have Freedom of Shape," Ger said.

"Exactly," Ilg said. "But he'll never understand. Now excuse me. I want to Think." And the oak tree was silent.

Pid laughed humorlessly. "The Men will kill you off," he said. "Just as they killed off all the other expeditions."

"No one from Grom has been killed," Ger told him. "The other expeditions are right here."

"Alive?"

"Certainly. The Men don't even know we exist. That Dog I was Hunting with is a Grom from the twelfth expedition. There are hundreds of us here, Pilot. We like it."

Pid tried to absorb it all. He had always known that the lower castes were lax in caste-consciousness. But this was preposterous!

This planet's secret menace was—freedom!

"Join us, Pilot," Ger said. "We've got a paradise here. Do you know how many species there are on this planet? An uncountable number! There's a shape to suit every need!"

Pid ignored them. Traitors!

He'd do the job all by himself.

So Men were unaware of the presence of the Grom. Getting near the reactor might not be so difficult after all. The others had failed in their duty because they were of the lower castes, weak and irresponsible. Even the Pilots among them must have been secretly sympathetic to the Cult of Shapelessness the Chief had mentioned, or the alien planet could never have swayed them.

What shape to assume for his attempt?

Pid considered.

A Dog might be best. Evidently Dogs could wander pretty much where they wished. If something went wrong, Pid could change his shape to meet the occasion.

"The Supreme Council will take care of all of you," he snarled, and shaped himself into a small brown Dog. "I'm going to set up the Displacer myself."

He studied himself for a moment, bared his teeth at Ger, and loped toward the gate.

He loped for about ten feet and stopped in utter horror.

The smells rushed at him from all directions. Smells in a profusion and variety he had never dreamed existed. Smells that were harsh, sweet, sharp, heavy, mysterious, overpowering. Smells that terrified. Alien and repulsive and inescapable, the odors of Earth struck him like a blow.

He curled his lips and held his breath. He ran on for a few steps, and had to breathe again. He almost choked.

He tried to remold his Dog-nostrils to be less sensitive. It didn't work. It wouldn't, so long as he kept the Dog-shape. An attempt to modify his metabolism didn't work either.

All this in the space of two or three seconds. He was rooted in his tracks, fighting the smells, wondering what to do.

Then the noises hit him.

They were a constant and staggering roar, through which every tiniest whisper of sound stood out clearly and distinct. Sounds upon sounds— more noise than he had ever heard before at one time in his life. The woods behind him had suddenly become a mad-house.

Utterly confused, he lost control and became Shapeless.

He half-ran, half-flowed into a nearby bush. There he re-Shaped, obliterating the offending Dog ears and nostrils with vicious strokes of his thoughts.

The Dog-shape was out. Absolutely. Such appalling sharpness of senses might be fine for a Hunter such as Ger—he probably gloried in them. But another moment of such impressions would have driven Pid the Pilot mad.

What now? He lay in the bush and thought about it, while gradually his mind threw off the last effects of the dizzying sensory assault.

He looked at the gate. The Men standing there evidently hadn't noticed his fiasco. They were looking in another direction.

... a Man?

Well, it was worth a try.

Studying the Men at the gate, Pid carefully shaped himself into a facsimile—a synthesis, actually, embodying one characteristic of that, another of this.

He emerged from the side of the bush opposite the gate, on his hands and knees. He sniffed the air, noting that the smells the Man-nostrils picked up weren't unpleasant at all. In fact, some of them were decidedly otherwise. It had just been the acuity of the Dog-nostrils, the number of smells they had detected and the near-brilliance with which they had done so, that had shocked him.

Also, the sounds weren't half so devastating. Only relatively close sounds stood out. All else was an undetailed whispering.

Evidently, Pid thought, it had been a long time since Men had been Hunters.

He tested his legs, standing up and taking a few clumsy steps. *Thud* of foot on ground. Drag the other leg forward in a heavy arc. *Thud*. Rocking from side to side, he marched back and forth behind the bush. His arms flapped as he sought balance. His head wobbled on its neck, until he remembered to hold it up. Head up, eyes down, he missed seeing a small rock. His heel turned on it. He sat down, hard.

The ankle hurt. Pid curled his Man-lips and crawled back into the bush.

The Man-shape was too unspeakably clumsy. It was offensive to plod one step at a time. Body held rigidly upright. Arms wobbling. There had been a deluge of sense-impressions in the Dog-shape; there was dull, stiff, half-alive inadequacy to the Man-shape.

Besides, it was dangerous, now that Pid thought it over, as well as distasteful. He couldn't control it properly. It wouldn't look right. Someone might question him. There was too much about Men he didn't— couldn't—know. The planting of the Displacer was too important a thing for him to fumble again. Only luck had kept him from being seen during the sensory onslaught.

The Displacer in his body pouch pulsed and tugged, urging him to be on his way toward the distant reactor room.

Grimly, Pid let out the last breath he had taken with his Man-lungs, and dissolved the lungs.

What shape to take?

Again he studied the gate, the Men standing beside it, the building beyond in which was the all-important reactor.

A small shape was needed. A fast one. An unobtrusive one.

He lay and thought.

The bush rustled above him. A small brown shape had fluttered down to light on a twig. It hopped to another twig, twittering. Then it fluttered off in a flash, and was gone.

That, Pid thought, was it.

A Sparrow that was not a Sparrow rose from the bush a few moments later. An observer would have seen it circle the bush, diving, hedgehopping, even looping, as if practicing all maneuvers possible to Sparrows.

Pid tensed his shoulder muscles, inclined his wings. He slipped off to the right, approached the bush at what seemed breakneck speed, though he knew this was only because of his small size. At the last second he lifted his tail. Not quite quickly enough. He swooped up and over the top of the bush, but his legs brushed the top leaves, his beak went down, and he stumbled in air for a few feet back-forward.

He blinked beady eyes as if at a challenge. Back toward the bush at a fine clip, again up and over. This time cleanly.

He chose a tree. Zoomed into its network of branches, wove a web of flight, working his way around and around the trunk, over and under branches that flashed before him, through crotches with no more than a feather's-breath to spare.

At last he rested on a low branch, and found himself chirping in delight.

The tree extruded a feeler from the branch he sat on, and touched his wings and tail.

"Interesting," said the tree. "I'll have to try that shape some time."

"Traitor," hissed Pid, growing a mouth in his chest to hiss it, and then he did something that caused Ilg to exclaim in outrage.

Pid flew out of the woods. Over the underbrush and across the open space toward the gate.

This body would do the trick!

This body would do anything!

He rose, in a matter of a few Sparrow heartbeats, to an altitude of a hundred feet. From here the gate, the Men, the building were small, sharp shapes against a green-brown mat. Pid found that he could see not only with unaccustomed clarity, but with a range of vision that astonished him. To right and to left he could see far into the hazy blue of the sky, and the higher he rose the farther he could see.

He rose higher.

The Displacer pulsed, reminding him of the job he had to do.

He stiffened his wings and glided, regretfully putting aside his desires to experiment with this wonderful shape, at least for the present. After he planted the Displacer, he would go off by himself for a while and do it just a little more—somewhere where Ilg and Ger would not see him—before the Grom Army arrived and the invasion began.

He felt a tiny twinge of guilt, as he circled. It was Evil to want to keep this alien flying shape any longer than was absolutely necessary to the performance of his duty. It was a device of the Shapeless One—

But what had Ilg said? All Grom are born Shapeless. It was true. Grom children were amorphous, until old enough to be instructed in the caste-shape of their ancestors.

Maybe it wasn't too great a sin to alter your Shape, then—just once in a long while. After all, one must be fully aware of the nature of Evil in order to meaningfully reject it.

He had fallen lower in circling. The Displacer pulse had strengthened. For some reason it irritated him. He drove higher on strong wings, circled again. Air rushed past him—a smooth, whispering flow, pierced by his beak, streaming invisibly past his sharp eyes, moving along his body in tiny turbulences that moved his feathers against his skin.

It occurred to him—or rather struck him with considerable force—that he was satisfying a longing of his Pilot Caste that went far deeper than Piloting.

He drove powerfully with his wings, felt tonus across his back, shot forward and up. He thought of the controls of his ship. He imagined flowing into them, becoming part of them, as he had so often done—and for the first time in his life the thought failed to excite him.

No machine could compare with this!

What he would give to have wings of his own!

... Get from my sight, Shapeless One!

The Displacer must be planted, activated. All Grom depended on him.

He eyed the building, far below. He would pass over it. The Displacer would tell him which window to enter—which window was so near the reactor that he could do his job before the Men even knew he was about.

He started to drop lower, and the Hawk struck.

It had been above him. His first inkling of danger was the sharp pain of talons in his back, and the stunning blow of a beak across his head.

Dazed, he let his back go Shapeless. His body-substance flowed from the grasp of the talons. He dropped a dozen feet and resumed Sparrow-shape, hearing an astonished squawk from the attacker.

He banked, and looked up. The Hawk was eyeing him.

Talons spread again. The sharp beak gaped. The Hawk swooped.

Pid had to fight as a Bird, naturally. He was four hundred feet above the ground.

So he became an impossibly deadly Bird.

He grew to twice the size of the Hawk. He grew a foot-long beak with a double razor's edge. He grew talons like six inch scimitars. His eyes gleamed a red challenge.

The Hawk broke flight, squalling in alarm. Frantically, tail down and widespread, it thundered its wings and came to a dead stop six feet from Pid.

Looking thoughtfully at Pid, it allowed itself to plummet. It fell a hundred feet, spread its wings, stretched its neck and flew off so hastily that its wings became blurs.

Pid saw no reason to pursue it.

Then, after a moment, he did.

He glided, keeping the Hawk in sight, thoughts racing, feeling the newness, the power, the wonder of Freedom of Shape.

Freedom....

He did not want to give it up.

The bird-shape was wondrous. He would experiment with it. Later, he might tire of it for a time and assume another—a crawling or running shape, or even a swimming one. The possibilities for excitement, for adventure, for fulfillment and simple sensual pleasure were endless!

Freedom of Shape was—obviously, now that you thought on it—the Grom birthright. And the caste-system was artificial—obviously. A device for political and priestly benefit—obviously.

Go away, Shapeless One ... this does not concern you.

He rose to a thousand feet, two thousand, three. The Displacer's pulse grew feebler and finally vanished.

At four thousand feet he released it and watched it spin downward, vanish into a cloud.

Then he set out after the Hawk, which was now only a dot on the horizon. He would find out how the Hawk had broken flight as it had—skidded on air—he wanted to do that too! There were so many things he wanted to learn about flying. In a week, he thought, he should be able to duplicate all the skill that millennia had evolved into Birds. Then his new life would really begin.

He became a torpedo-shape with huge wings, and sped after the Hawk.

Death Wish

Illustrated by WEISS

Compared with a spaceship in distress, going to hell in a handbasket is roomy and slow!

The space freighter *Queen Dierdre* was a great, squat, pockmarked vessel of the Earth-Mars run and she never gave anyone a bit of trouble. That should have been sufficient warning to Mr. Watkins, her engineer. Watkins was fond of saying that there are two kinds of equipment—the kind that fails bit by bit, and the kind that fails all at once.

Watkins was short and red-faced, magnificently mustached, and always a little out of breath. With a cigar in his hand, over a glass of beer, he talked most cynically about his ship, in the immemorial fashion of engineers. But in reality, Watkins was foolishly infatuated with *Dierdre*, idealized her, humanized her, and couldn't conceive of anything serious ever happening.

On this particular run, *Dierdre* soared away from Terra at the proper speed; Mr. Watkins signaled that fuel was being consumed at the proper rate; and Captain Somers cut the engines at the proper moment indicated by Mr. Rajcik, the navigator.

As soon as Point Able had been reached and the engines stopped, Somers frowned and studied his complex control board. He was a thin and meticulous man, and he operated his ship with mechanical perfection. He was well liked in the front offices of Mikkelsen Space Lines, where Old Man Mikkelsen pointed to Captain Somers' reports as models of neatness and efficiency. On Mars, he stayed at the Officers' Club, eschewing the stews and dives of Marsport. On Earth, he lived in a little Vermont cottage and enjoyed the quiet companionship of two cats, a Japanese houseboy, and a wife.

His instructions read true. And yet he sensed something wrong. Somers knew every creak, rattle and groan that *Dierdre* was capable of making. During blastoff, he had heard something *different*. In space, something different had to be wrong.

"Mr. Rajcik," he said, turning to his navigator, "would you check the cargo? I believe something may have shifted."

"You bet," Rajcik said cheerfully. He was an almost offensively handsome young man with black wavy hair, blasé blue eyes and a cleft chin. Despite his appearance, Rajcik was thoroughly qualified for his position. But he was only one of fifty thousand thoroughly qualified men who lusted for a berth on one of the fourteen spaceships in existence. Only Stephen Rajcik had had the foresight, appearance and fortitude to court and wed Helga, Old Man Mikkelsen's eldest daughter.

Rajcik went aft to the cargo hold. *Dierdre* was carrying transistors this time, and microfilm books, platinum filaments, salamis, and other items that could not as yet be produced on Mars. But the bulk of her space was taken by the immense Fahrensen Computer.

Rajcik checked the positioning lines on the monster, examined the stays and turnbuckles that held it in place, and returned to the cabin.

"All in order, Boss," he reported to Captain Somers, with the smile that only an employer's son-in-law can both manage and afford.

"Mr. Watkins, do you read anything?"

Watkins was at his own instrument panel. "Not a thing, sir. I'll vouch for every bit of equipment in *Dierdre*."

"Very well. How long before we reach Point Baker?"

"Three minutes, Chief," Rajcik said.

"Good."

The spaceship hung in the void, all sensation of speed lost for lack of a reference point. Beyond the portholes was darkness, the true color of the Universe, perforated by the brilliant lost points of the stars.

Captain Somers turned away from the disturbing reminder of his extreme finitude and wondered if he could land *Dierdre* without shifting the computer. It was by far the largest, heaviest and most delicate piece of equipment ever transported in space.

He worried about that machine. Its value ran into the billions of dollars, for Mars Colony had ordered the best possible, a machine whose utility would offset the immense transportation charge across space. As a result, the Fahrensen Computer was perhaps the most complex and advanced machine ever built by Man.

"Ten seconds to Point Baker," Rajcik announced.

"Very well." Somers readied himself at the control board.

"Four—three—two—one—fire!"

Somers activated the engines. Acceleration pressed the three men back into their couches, and more acceleration, and—shockingly—still more acceleration.

"The fuel!" Watkins yelped, watching his indicators spinning.

"The course!" Rajcik gasped, fighting for breath.

Captain Somers cut the engine switch. The engines continued firing, pressing the men deeper into their couches. The cabin lights flickered, went out, came on again.

And still the acceleration mounted and *Dierdre's* engines howled in agony, thrusting the ship forward. Somers raised one leaden hand and inched it toward the emergency cut-off switch. With a fantastic expenditure of energy, he reached the switch, depressed it.

The engines stopped with dramatic suddenness, while tortured metal creaked and groaned. The lights flickered rapidly, as though *Dierdre* were blinking in pain. They steadied and then there was silence.

Watkins hurried to the engine room. He returned morosely.

"Of all the damn things," he muttered.

"What was it?" Captain Somers asked.

"Main firing circuit. It fused on us." He shook his head. "Metal fatigue, I'd say. It must have been flawed for years."

"When was it last checked out?"

"Well, it's a sealed unit. Supposed to outlast the ship. Absolutely fool-proof, unless—"

"Unless it's flawed."

"Don't blame it on me! Those circuits are supposed to be X-rayed, heat-treated, fluoroscoped—you just can't trust machinery!"

At last Watkins believed that engineering axiom.

"How are we on fuel?" Captain Somers asked.

"Not enough left to push a kiddy car down Main Street," Watkins said gloomily. "If I could get my hands on that factory inspector ..."

Captain Somers turned to Rajcik, who was seated at the navigator's desk, hunched over his charts. "How does this affect our course?"

Rajcik finished the computation he was working on and gnawed thoughtfully at his pencil.

"It kills us. We're going to cross the orbit of Mars before Mars gets there."

"How long before?"

"Too long. Captain, we're flying out of the Solar System like the prover-bial bat out of hell."

Rajcik smiled, a courageous, devil-may-care smile which Watkins found singularly inappropriate.

"Damn it, man," he roared, "don't just leave it there. We've got a little fuel left. We can turn her, can't we? You are a navigator, aren't you?"

"I am," Rajcik said icily. "And if I computed my courses the way you maintain your engines, we'd be plowing through Australia now."

"Why, you little company toady! At least I got my job legitimately, not by marrying—"

"That's enough!" Captain Somers cut in.

Watkins, his face a mottled red, his mustache bristling, looked like a walrus about to charge. And Rajcik, eyes glittering, was waiting hope-fully.

"No more of this," Somers said. "I give the orders here."

"Then give some!" Watkins snapped. "Tell him to plot a return curve. This is life or death!"

"All the more reason for remaining cool. Mr. Rajcik, can you plot such a course?"

"First thing I tried," Rajcik said. "Not a chance, on the fuel we have left. We can turn a degree or two, but it won't help."

Watkins said, "Of course it will! We'll curve back into the Solar System!"

"Sure, but the best curve we can make will take a few thousand years for us to complete."

"Perhaps a landfall on some other planet—Neptune, Uranus—"

Rajcik shook his head. "Even if an outer planet were in the right place at the right time, we'd need fuel—a lot of fuel—to get into a braking orbit. And if we could, who'd come get us? No ship has gone past Mars yet."

"At least we'd have a chance," Watkins said.

"Maybe," Rajcik agreed indifferently. "But we can't swing it. I'm afraid you'll have to kiss the Solar System good-by."

Captain Somers wiped his forehead and tried to think of a plan. He found it difficult to concentrate. There was too great a discrepancy between his knowledge of the situation and its appearance. He knew—intellectually—that his ship was traveling out of the Solar System at a tremendous rate of speed. But in appearance they were stationary, hung in the abyss, three men trapped in a small, hot room, breathing the smell of hot metal and perspiration.

"What shall we do, Captain?" Watkins asked.

Somers frowned at the engineer. Did the man expect him to pull a solution out of the air? How was he even supposed to concentrate on the problem? He had to slow the ship, turn it. But his senses told him that the ship was not moving. How, then, could speed constitute a problem?

He couldn't help but feel that the real problem was to get away from these high-strung, squabbling men, to escape from this hot, smelly little room.

"Captain! You must have some idea!"

Somers tried to shake his feeling of unreality. The problem, the real problem, he told himself, was how to stop the ship.

He looked around the fixed cabin and out the porthole at the unmoving stars. *We are moving very rapidly,* he thought, unconvinced.

Rajcik said disgustedly, "Our noble captain can't face the situation."

"Of course I can," Somers objected, feeling very light-headed and unreal. "I can pilot any course you lay down. That's my only real responsibility. Plot us a course to Mars!"

"Sure!" Rajcik said, laughing. "I can! I will! Engineer, I'm going to need plenty of fuel for this course—about ten tons! See that I get it!"

"Right you are," said Watkins. "Captain, I'd like to put in a requisition for ten tons of fuel."

"Requisition granted," Somers said. "All right, gentlemen, responsibility is inevitably circular. Let's get a grip on ourselves. Mr. Rajcik, suppose you radio Mars."

When contact had been established, Somers took the microphone and stated their situation. The company official at the other end seemed to have trouble grasping it.

"But can't you turn the ship?" he asked bewilderedly. "Any kind of an orbit—"

"No. I've just explained that."

"Then what do you propose to do, Captain?"

"That's exactly what I'm asking you."

There was a babble of voices from the loudspeaker, punctuated by bursts of static. The lights flickered and reception began to fade. Rajcik, working frantically, managed to re-establish the contact.

"Captain," the official on Mars said, "we can't think of a thing. If you could swing into any sort of an orbit—"

"I can't!"

"Under the circumstances, you have the right to try anything at all. Anything, Captain!"

Somers groaned. "Listen, I can think of just one thing. We could bail out in spacesuits as near Mars as possible. Link ourselves together, take the portable transmitter. It wouldn't give much of a signal, but you'd know our approximate position. Everything would have to be figured pretty closely—those suits just carry twelve hours' air—but it's a chance."

There was a confusion of voices from the other end. Then the official said, "I'm sorry, Captain."

"What? I'm telling you it's our one chance!"

"Captain, the only ship on Mars now is the Diana. Her engines are being overhauled."

"How long before she can be spaceborne?"

"Three weeks, at least. And a ship from Earth would take too long. Captain, I wish we could think of something. About the only thing we can suggest—"

The reception suddenly failed again.

Rajcik cursed frustratedly as he worked over the radio. Watkins gnawed at his mustache. Somers glanced out a porthole and looked hurriedly away, for the stars, their destination, were impossibly distant.

They heard static again, faintly now.

"I can't get much more," Rajcik said. "This damned reception.... What could they have been suggesting?"

"Whatever it was," said Watkins, "they didn't think it would work."

"What the hell does that matter?" Rajcik asked, annoyed. "It'd give us something to do."

They heard the official's voice, a whisper across space.

"Can you hear ... Suggest ..."

At full amplification, the voice faded, then returned. "Can only suggest ... most unlikely ... but try ... calculator ... try ..."

The voice was gone. And then even the static was gone.

"That does it," Rajcik said. "The calculator? Did he mean the Fahrensen

Computer in our hold?"

"I see what he meant," said Captain Somers. "The Fahrensen is a very advanced job. No one knows the limits of its potential. He suggests we present our problem to it."

"That's ridiculous," Watkins snorted. "This problem has no solution."

"It doesn't seem to," Somers agreed. "But the big computers have solved other apparently impossible problems. We can't lose anything by trying."

"No," said Rajcik, "as long as we don't pin any hopes on it."

"That's right. We don't dare hope. Mr. Watkins, I believe this is your department."

"Oh, what's the use?" Watkins asked. "You say don't hope—but both of you are hoping anyhow! You think the big electronic god is going to save your lives. Well, it's not!"

"We have to try," Somers told him.

"We don't! I wouldn't give it the satisfaction of turning us down!"

They stared at him in vacant astonishment.

"Now you're implying that machines think," said Rajcik.

"Of course I am," Watkins said. "Because they do! No, I'm not out of my head. Any engineer will tell you that a complex machine has a personality all its own. Do you know what that personality is like? Cold, withdrawn, uncaring, unfeeling. A machine's only purpose is to frustrate desire and produce two problems for everyone it solves. And do you know why a machine feels this way?"

"You're hysterical," Somers told him.

"I am not. A machine feels this way because it knows it is an unnatural creation in nature's domain. Therefore it wishes to reach entropy and cease—a

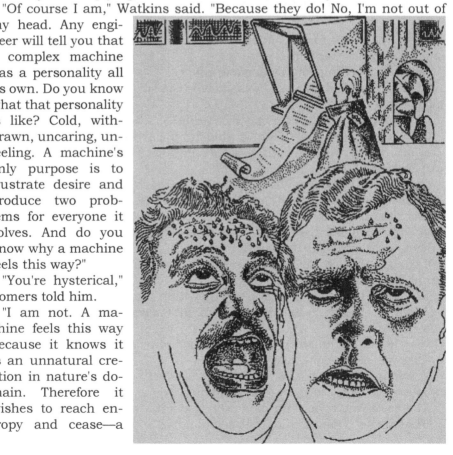

mechanical death wish."

"I've never heard such gibberish in my life," Somers said. "Are you going to hook up that computer?"

"Of course. I'm a human. I keep trying. I just wanted you to understand fully that there is no hope." He went to the cargo hold.

After he had gone, Rajcik grinned and shook his head. "We'd better watch him."

"He'll be all right," Somers said.

"Maybe, maybe not." Rajcik pursed his lips thoughtfully. "He's blaming the situation on a machine personality now, trying to absolve himself of guilt. And it is his fault that we're in this spot. An engineer is responsible for all equipment."

"I don't believe you can put the blame on him so dogmatically," Somers replied.

"Sure I can," Rajcik said. "I personally don't care, though. This is as good a way to die as any other and better than most."

Captain Somers wiped perspiration from his face. Again the notion came to him that the problem—the real problem—was to find a way out of this hot, smelly, motionless little box.

Rajcik said, "Death in space is an appealing idea, in certain ways. Imagine an entire spaceship for your tomb! And you have a variety of ways of actually dying. Thirst and starvation I rule out as unimaginative. But there are possibilities in heat, cold, implosion, explosion—"

"This is pretty morbid," Somers said.

"I'm a pretty morbid fellow," Rajcik said carelessly. "But at least I'm not blaming inanimate objects, the way Watkins is. Or permitting myself the luxury of shock, like you." He studied Somers' face. "This is your first real emergency, isn't it, Captain?"

"I suppose so," Somers answered vaguely.

"And you're responding to it like a stunned ox," Rajcik said. "Wake up, Captain! If you can't live with joy, at least try to extract some pleasure from your dying."

"Shut up," Somers said, with no heat. "Why don't you read a book or something?"

"I've read all the books on board. I have nothing to distract me except an analysis of your character."

Watkins returned to the cabin. "Well, I've activated your big electronic god. Would anyone care to make a burned offering in front of it?"

"Have you given it the problem?"

"Not yet. I decided to confer with the high priest. What shall I request of the demon, sir?"

"Give it all the data you can," Somers said. "Fuel, oxygen, water, food—that sort of thing. Then tell it we want to return to Earth. Alive," he added.

"It'll love that," Watkins said. "It'll get such pleasure out of rejecting our problem as unsolvable. Or better yet—insufficient data. In that way, it can hint that a solution is possible, but just outside our reach. It can keep us hoping."

Somers and Rajcik followed him to the cargo hold. The computer, activated now, hummed softly. Lights flashed swiftly over its panels, blue and white and red.

Watkins punched buttons and turned dials for fifteen minutes, then moved back.

"Watch for the red light on top," he said. "That means the problem is rejected."

"Don't say it," Rajcik warned quickly.

Watkins laughed. "Superstitious little fellow, aren't you?"

"But not incompetent," Rajcik said, smiling.

"Can't you two quit it?" Somers demanded, and both men turned startedly to face him.

"Behold!" Rajcik said. "The sleeper has awakened."

"After a fashion," said Watkins, snickering.

Somers suddenly felt that if death or rescue did not come quickly, they would kill each other, or drive each other crazy.

"Look!" Rajcik said.

A light on the computer's panel was flashing green.

"Must be a mistake," said Watkins. "Green means the problem is solvable within the conditions set down."

"Solvable!" Rajcik said.

"But it's impossible," Watkins argued. "It's fooling us, leading us on—"

"Don't be superstitious," Rajcik mocked. "How soon do we get the solution?"

"It's coming now." Watkins pointed to a paper tape inching out of a slot in the machine's face. "But there must be something wrong!"

They watched as, millimeter by millimeter, the tape crept out. The computer hummed, its lights flashing green. Then the hum stopped. The green lights blazed once more and faded.

"What happened?" Rajcik wanted to know.

"It's finished," Watkins said.

"Pick it up! Read it!"

"You read it. You won't get me to play its game."

Rajcik laughed nervously and rubbed his hands together, but didn't move. Both men turned to Somers.

"Captain, it's your responsibility."

"Go ahead, Captain!"

Somers looked with loathing at his engineer and navigator. His responsibility, everything was his responsibility. Would they never leave him alone?

He went up to the machine, pulled the tape free, read it with slow deliberation.

"What does it say, sir?" Rajcik asked.

"Is it—possible?" Watkins urged.

"Oh, yes," Somers said. "It's possible." He laughed and looked around at the hot, smelly, low-ceilinged little room with its locked doors and windows.

"What is it?" Rajcik shouted.

Somers said, "You figured a few thousand years to return to the Solar System, Rajcik? Well, the computer agrees with you. Twenty-three hundred years, to be precise. Therefore, it has given us a suitable longevity serum."

"Twenty-three hundred years," Rajcik mumbled. "I suppose we hibernate or something of the sort."

"Not at all," Somers said calmly. "As a matter of fact, this serum does away quite nicely with the need for sleep. We stay awake and watch each other."

The three men looked at one another and at the sickeningly familiar room smelling of metal and perspiration, its sealed doors and windows that stared at an unchanging spectacle of stars.

Watkins said, "Yes, that's the sort of thing it would do."

WATCHBIRD

Illustrated by EMSH

Strange how often the Millennium has been at hand. The idea is peace on Earth, see, and the way to do it is by figuring out angles.

When Gelsen entered, he saw that the rest of the watchbird manufacturers were already present. There were six of them, not counting himself, and the room was blue with expensive cigar smoke.

"Hi, Charlie," one of them called as he came in.

The rest broke off conversation long enough to wave a casual greeting at him. As a watchbird manufacturer, he was a member manufacturer of salvation, he reminded himself wryly. Very exclusive. You must have a certified government contract if you want to save the human race.

"The government representative isn't here yet," one of the men told him. "He's due any minute."

"We're getting the green light," another said.

"Fine." Gelsen found a chair near the door and looked around the room. It was like a convention, or a Boy Scout rally. The six men made up for their lack of numbers by sheer volume. The president of Southern Consolidated was talking at the top of his lungs about watchbird's enormous durability. The two presidents he was talking at were grinning, nodding, one trying to interrupt with the results of a test he had run on watchbird's resourcefulness, the other talking about the new recharging apparatus.

The other three men were in their own little group, delivering what sounded like a panegyric to watchbird.

Gelsen noticed that all of them stood straight and tall, like the saviors they felt they were. He didn't find it funny. Up to a few days ago he had felt that way himself. He had considered himself a pot-bellied, slightly balding saint.

He sighed and lighted a cigarette. At the beginning of the project, he had been as enthusiastic as the others. He remembered saying to Macintyre, his chief engineer, "Mac, a new day is coming. Watchbird is the Answer." And Macintyre had nodded very profoundly—another watchbird convert.

How wonderful it had seemed then! A simple, reliable answer to one of mankind's greatest problems, all wrapped and packaged in a pound of incorruptible metal, crystal and plastics.

Perhaps that was the very reason he was doubting it now. Gelsen suspected that you don't solve human problems so easily. There had to be a catch somewhere.

After all, murder was an old problem, and watchbird too new a solution.

"Gentlemen—" They had been talking so heatedly that they hadn't noticed the government representative entering. Now the room became quiet at once.

"Gentlemen," the plump government man said, "the President, with the consent of Congress, has acted to form a watchbird division for every city and town in the country."

The men burst into a spontaneous shout of triumph. They were going to have their chance to save the world after all, Gelsen thought, and worriedly asked himself what was wrong with that.

He listened carefully as the government man outlined the distribution scheme. The country was to be divided into seven areas, each to be supplied and serviced by one manufacturer. This meant monopoly, of course, but a necessary one. Like the telephone service, it was in the public's best interests. You couldn't have competition in watchbird service. Watchbird was for everyone.

"The President hopes," the representative continued, "that full watchbird service will be installed in the shortest possible time. You will have top priorities on strategic metals, manpower, and so forth."

"Speaking for myself," the president of Southern Consolidated said, "I expect to have the first batch of watchbirds distributed within the week. Production is all set up."

The rest of the men were equally ready. The factories had been prepared to roll out the watchbirds for months now. The final standardized equipment had been agreed upon, and only the Presidential go-ahead had been lacking.

"Fine," the representative said. "If that is all, I think we can—is there a question?"

"Yes, sir," Gelsen said. "I want to know if the present model is the one we are going to manufacture."

"Of course," the representative said. "It's the most advanced."

"I have an objection." Gelsen stood up. His colleagues were glaring coldly at him. Obviously he was delaying the advent of the golden age.

"What is your objection?" the representative asked.

"First, let me say that I am one hundred per cent in favor of a machine to stop murder. It's been needed for a long time. I object only to the watchbird's learning circuits. They serve, in effect, to animate the machine and give it a pseudo-consciousness. I can't approve of that."

"But, Mr. Gelsen, you yourself testified that the watchbird would not be completely efficient unless such circuits were introduced. Without them, the watchbirds could stop only an estimated seventy per cent of murders."

"I know that," Gelsen said, feeling extremely uncomfortable. "I believe there might be a moral danger in allowing a machine to make decisions that are rightfully Man's," he declared doggedly.

"Oh, come now, Gelsen," one of the corporation presidents said. "It's nothing of the sort. The watchbird will only reinforce the decisions made by honest men from the beginning of time."

"I think that is true," the representative agreed. "But I can understand how Mr. Gelsen feels. It is sad that we must put a human problem into the hands of a machine, sadder still that we must have a machine enforce our laws. But I ask you to remember, Mr. Gelsen, that there is no other possible way of stopping a murderer before he strikes. It would be unfair to the many innocent people killed every year if we were to restrict watchbird on philosophical grounds. Don't you agree that I'm right?"

"Yes, I suppose I do," Gelsen said unhappily. He had told himself all that a thousand times, but something still bothered him. Perhaps he would talk it over with Macintyre.

As the conference broke up, a thought struck him. He grinned.

A lot of policemen were going to be out of work!

"Now what do you think of that?" Officer Celtrics demanded. "Fifteen years in Homicide and a machine is replacing me." He wiped a large red hand across his forehead and leaned against the captain's desk. "Ain't science marvelous?"

Two other policemen, late of Homicide, nodded glumly.

"Don't worry about it," the captain said. "We'll find a home for you in Larceny, Celtrics. You'll like it here."

"I just can't get over it," Celtrics complained. "A lousy little piece of tin and glass is going to solve all the crimes."

"Not quite," the captain said. "The watchbirds are supposed to prevent the crimes before they happen."

"Then how'll they be crimes?" one of the policeman asked. "I mean they can't hang you for murder until you commit one, can they?"

"That's not the idea," the captain said. "The watchbirds are supposed to stop a man before he commits a murder."

"Then no one arrests him?" Celtrics asked.

"I don't know how they're going to work that out," the captain admitted.

The men were silent for a while. The captain yawned and examined his watch.

"The thing I don't understand," Celtrics said, still leaning on the captain's desk, "is just how do they do it? How did it start, Captain?"

The captain studied Celtrics' face for possible irony; after all, watchbird had been in the papers for months. But then he remembered that

Celtrics, like his sidekicks, rarely bothered to turn past the sports pages.

"Well," the captain said, trying to remember what he had read in the Sunday supplements, "these scientists were working on criminology. They were studying murderers, to find out what made them tick. So they found that murderers throw out a different sort of brain wave from ordinary people. And their glands act funny, too. All this happens when they're about to commit a murder. So these scientists worked out a special machine to flash red or something when these brain waves turned on."

"Scientists," Celtrics said bitterly.

"Well, after the scientists had this machine, they didn't know what to do with it. It was too big to move around, and murderers didn't drop in often enough to make it flash. So they built it into a smaller unit and tried it out in a few police stations. I think they tried one upstate. But it didn't work so good. You couldn't get to the crime in time. That's why they built the watchbirds."

"I don't think they'll stop no criminals," one of the policemen insisted.

"They sure will. I read the test results. They can smell him out before he commits a crime. And when they reach him, they give him a powerful shock or something. It'll stop him."

"You closing up Homicide, Captain?" Celtrics asked.

"Nope," the captain said. "I'm leaving a skeleton crew in until we see how these birds do."

"Hah," Celtrics said. "Skeleton crew. That's funny."

"Sure," the captain said. "Anyhow, I'm going to leave some men on. It seems the birds don't stop all murders."

"Why not?"

"Some murderers don't have these brain waves," the captain answered, trying to remember what the newspaper article had said. "Or their glands don't work or something."

"Which ones don't they stop?" Celtrics asked, with professional curiosity.

"I don't know. But I hear they got the damned things fixed so they're going to stop all of them soon."

"How they working that?"

"They learn. The watchbirds, I mean. Just like people."

"You kidding me?"

"Nope."

"Well," Celtrics said, "I think I'll just keep old Betsy oiled, just in case. You can't trust these scientists."

"Right."

"Birds!" Celtrics scoffed.

Over the town, the watchbird soared in a long, lazy curve. Its aluminum hide glistened in the morning sun, and dots of light danced on its stiff wings. Silently it flew.

Silently, but with all senses functioning. Built-in kinesthetics told the watchbird where it was, and held it in a long search curve. Its eyes and ears operated as one unit, searching, seeking.

And then something happened! The watchbird's electronically fast reflexes picked up the edge of a sensation. A correlation center tested it, matching it with electrical and chemical data in its memory files. A relay tripped.

Down the watchbird spiraled, coming in on the increasingly strong sensation. It smelled the outpouring of certain glands, tasted a deviant brain wave.

Fully alerted and armed, it spun and banked in the bright morning sunlight.

Dinelli was so intent he didn't see the watchbird coming. He had his gun poised, and his eyes pleaded with the big grocer.

"Don't come no closer."

"You lousy little punk," the grocer said, and took another step forward. "Rob me? I'll break every bone in your puny body."

The grocer, too stupid or too courageous to understand the threat of the gun, advanced on the little thief.

"All right," Dinelli said, in a thorough state of panic. "All right, sucker, take—"

A bolt of electricity knocked him on his back. The gun went off, smashing a breakfast food display.

"What in hell?" the grocer asked, staring at the stunned thief. And then he saw a flash of silver wings. "Well, I'm really damned. Those watchbirds work!"

He stared until, the wings disappeared in the sky. Then he telephoned the police.

The watchbird returned to his search curve. His thinking center correlated the new facts he had learned about murder. Several of these he hadn't known before.

This new information was simultaneously flashed to all the other watchbirds and their information was flashed back to him.

New information, methods, definitions were constantly passing between them.

Now that the watchbirds were rolling off the assembly line in a steady stream, Gelsen allowed himself to relax. A loud contented hum filled his plant. Orders were being filled on time, with top priorities given to the biggest cities in his area, and working down to the smallest towns.

"All smooth, Chief," Macintyre said, coming in the door. He had just completed a routine inspection.

"Fine. Have a seat."

The big engineer sat down and lighted a cigarette.

"We've been working on this for some time," Gelsen said, when he couldn't think of anything else.

"We sure have," Macintyre agreed. He leaned back and inhaled deeply. He had been one of the consulting engineers on the original watchbird. That was six years back. He had been working for Gelsen ever since, and the men had become good friends.

"The thing I wanted to ask you was this—" Gelsen paused. He couldn't think how to phrase what he wanted. Instead he asked, "What do you think of the watchbirds, Mac?"

"Who, me?" The engineer grinned nervously. He had been eating, drinking and sleeping watchbird ever since its inception. He had never found it necessary to have an attitude. "Why, I think it's great."

"I don't mean that," Gelsen said. He realized that what he wanted was to have someone understand his point of view. "I mean do you figure there might be some danger in machine thinking?"

"I don't think so, Chief. Why do you ask?"

"Look, I'm no scientist or engineer. I've just handled cost and production and let you boys worry about how. But as a layman, watchbird is starting to frighten me."

"No reason for that."

"I don't like the idea of the learning circuits."

"But why not?" Then Macintyre grinned again. "I know. You're like a lot of people, Chief—afraid your machines are going to wake up and say, 'What are we doing here? Let's go out and rule the world.' Is that it?"

"Maybe something like that," Gelsen admitted.

"No chance of it," Macintyre said. "The watchbirds are complex, I'll admit, but an M.I.T. calculator is a whole lot more complex. And it hasn't got consciousness."

"No. But the watchbirds can learn."

"Sure. So can all the new calculators. Do you think they'll team up with the watchbirds?"

Gelsen felt annoyed at Macintyre, and even more annoyed at himself for being ridiculous. "It's a fact that the watchbirds can put their learning into action. No one is monitoring them."

"So that's the trouble," Macintyre said.

"I've been thinking of getting out of watchbird." Gelsen hadn't realized it until that moment.

"Look, Chief," Macintyre said. "Will you take an engineer's word on this?"

"Let's hear it."

"The watchbirds are no more dangerous than an automobile, an IBM calculator or a thermometer. They have no more consciousness or volition than those things. The watchbirds are built to respond to certain stimuli, and to carry out certain operations when they receive that stimuli."

"And the learning circuits?"

"You have to have those," Macintyre said patiently, as though explaining the whole thing to a ten-year-old. "The purpose of the watchbird is to frustrate all murder-attempts, right? Well, only certain murderers give out these stimuli. In order to stop all of them, the watchbird has to search out new definitions of murder and correlate them with what it already knows."

"I think it's inhuman," Gelsen said.

"That's the best thing about it. The watchbirds are unemotional. Their reasoning is non-anthropomorphic. You can't bribe them or drug them. You shouldn't fear them, either."

The intercom on Gelsen's desk buzzed. He ignored it.

"I know all this," Gelsen said. "But, still, sometimes I feel like the man who invented dynamite. He thought it would only be used for blowing up tree stumps."

"You didn't invent watchbird."

"I still feel morally responsible because I manufacture them."

The intercom buzzed again, and Gelsen irritably punched a button.

"The reports are in on the first week of watchbird operation," his secretary told him.

"How do they look?"

"Wonderful, sir."

"Send them in in fifteen minutes." Gelsen switched the intercom off and turned back to Macintyre, who was cleaning his fingernails with a wooden match. "Don't you think that this represents a trend in human thinking? The mechanical god? The electronic father?"

"Chief," Macintyre said, "I think you should study watchbird more closely. Do you know what's built into the circuits?"

"Only generally."

"First, there is a purpose. Which is to stop living organisms from committing murder. Two, murder may be defined as an act of violence, consisting of breaking, mangling, maltreating or otherwise stopping the functions of a living organism by a living organism. Three, most murderers are detectable by certain chemical and electrical changes."

Macintyre paused to light another cigarette. "Those conditions take care of the routine functions. Then, for the learning circuits, there are two more conditions. Four, there are some living organisms who commit murder without the signs mentioned in three. Five, these can be detected by data applicable to condition two."

"I see," Gelsen said.

"You realize how foolproof it is?"

"I suppose so." Gelsen hesitated a moment. "I guess that's all."

"Right," the engineer said, and left.

Gelsen thought for a few moments. There couldn't be anything wrong with the watchbirds.

"Send in the reports," he said into the intercom.

High above the lighted buildings of the city, the watchbird soared. It was dark, but in the distance the watchbird could see another, and another beyond that. For this was a large city.

To prevent murder ...

There was more to watch for now. New information had crossed the invisible network that connected all watchbirds. New data, new ways of detecting the violence of murder.

There! The edge of a sensation! Two watchbirds dipped simultaneously. One had received the scent a fraction of a second before the other. He continued down while the other resumed monitoring.

Condition four, there are some living organisms who commit murder without the signs mentioned in condition three.

Through his new information, the watchbird knew by extrapolation that this organism was bent on murder, even though the characteristic chemical and electrical smells were absent.

The watchbird, all senses acute, closed in on the organism. He found what he wanted, and dived.

Roger Greco leaned against a building, his hands in his pockets. In his left hand was the cool butt of a .45. Greco waited patiently.

He wasn't thinking of anything in particular, just relaxing against a building, waiting for a man. Greco didn't know why the man was to be killed. He didn't care. Greco's lack of curiosity was part of his value. The other part was his skill.

One bullet, neatly placed in the head of a man he didn't know. It didn't excite him or sicken him. It was a job, just like anything else. You killed a man. So?

As Greco's victim stepped out of a building, Greco lifted the .45 out of his pocket. He released the safety and braced the gun with his right hand. He still wasn't thinking of anything as he took aim ...

And was knocked off his feet.

Greco thought he had been shot. He struggled up again, looked around, and sighted foggily on his victim.

Again he was knocked down.

This time he lay on the ground, trying to draw a bead. He never thought of stopping, for Greco was a craftsman.

With the next blow, everything went black. Permanently, because the watchbird's duty was to protect the object of violence—*at whatever cost to the murderer.*

The victim walked to his car. He hadn't noticed anything unusual. Everything had happened in silence.

Gelsen was feeling pretty good. The watchbirds had been operating perfectly. Crimes of violence had been cut in half, and cut again. Dark alleys were no longer mouths of horror. Parks and playgrounds were not places to shun after dusk.

Of course, there were still robberies. Petty thievery flourished, and embezzlement, larceny, forgery and a hundred other crimes.

But that wasn't so important. You could regain lost money—never a lost life.

Gelsen was ready to admit that he had been wrong about the watchbirds. They were doing a job that humans had been unable to accomplish.

The first hint of something wrong came that morning.

Macintyre came into his office. He stood silently in front of Gelsen's desk, looking annoyed and a little embarrassed.

"What's the matter, Mac?" Gelsen asked.

"One of the watchbirds went to work on a slaughterhouse man. Knocked him out."

Gelsen thought about it for a moment. Yes, the watchbirds would do that. With their new learning circuits, they had probably defined the killing of animals as murder.

"Tell the packers to mechanize their slaughtering," Gelsen said. "I never liked that business myself."

"All right," Macintyre said. He pursed his lips, then shrugged his shoulders and left.

Gelsen stood beside his desk, thinking. Couldn't the watchbirds differentiate between a murderer and a man engaged in a legitimate profession? No, evidently not. To them, murder was murder. No exceptions. He frowned. That might take a little ironing out in the circuits.

But not too much, he decided hastily. Just make them a little more discriminating.

He sat down again and buried himself in paperwork, trying to avoid the edge of an old fear.

They strapped the prisoner into the chair and fitted the electrode to his leg.

"Oh, oh," he moaned, only half-conscious now of what they were doing.

They fitted the helmet over his shaved head and tightened the last straps. He continued to moan softly.

And then the watchbird swept in. How he had come, no one knew. Prisons are large and strong, with many locked doors, but the watchbird was there—

To stop a murder.

"Get that thing out of here!" the warden shouted, and reached for the switch. The watchbird knocked him down.

"Stop that!" a guard screamed, and grabbed for the switch himself. He was knocked to the floor beside the warden.

"This isn't murder, you idiot!" another guard said. He drew his gun to shoot down the glittering, wheeling metal bird.

Anticipating, the watchbird smashed him back against the wall.

There was silence in the room. After a while, the man in the helmet started to giggle. Then he stopped.

The watchbird stood on guard, fluttering in mid-air—

Making sure no murder was done.

New data flashed along the watchbird network. Unmonitored, independent, the thousands of watchbirds received and acted upon it.

The breaking, mangling or otherwise stopping the functions of a living organism by a living organism. New acts to stop.

"Damn you, git going!" Farmer Ollister shouted, and raised his whip again. The horse balked, and the wagon rattled and shook as he edged sideways.

"You lousy hunk of pigmeal, git going!" the farmer yelled and he raised the whip again.

It never fell. An alert watchbird, sensing violence, had knocked him out of his seat.

A living organism? What is a living organism? The watchbirds extended their definitions as they became aware of more facts. And, of course, this gave them more work.

The deer was just visible at the edge of the woods. The hunter raised his rifle, and took careful aim.

He didn't have time to shoot.

With his free hand, Gelsen mopped perspiration from his face. "All right," he said into the telephone. He listened to the stream of vituperation from the other end, then placed the receiver gently in its cradle.

"What was that one?" Macintyre asked. He was unshaven, tie loose, shirt unbuttoned.

"Another fisherman," Gelsen said. "It seems the watchbirds won't let him fish even though his family is starving. What are we going to do about it, he wants to know."

"How many hundred is that?"

"I don't know. I haven't opened the mail."

"Well, I figured out where the trouble is," Macintyre said gloomily, with the air of a man who knows just how he blew up the Earth—after it was too late.

"Let's hear it."

"Everybody took it for granted that we wanted all murder stopped. We figured the watchbirds would think as we do. We ought to have qualified the conditions."

"I've got an idea," Gelsen said, "that we'd have to know just why and what murder is, before we could qualify the conditions properly. And if we knew that, we wouldn't need the watchbirds."

"Oh, I don't know about that. They just have to be told that some things which look like murder are not murder."

"But why should they stop fisherman?" Gelsen asked.

"Why shouldn't they? Fish and animals are living organisms. We just don't think that killing them is murder."

The telephone rang. Gelsen glared at it and punched the intercom. "I told you no more calls, no matter what."

"This is from Washington," his secretary said. "I thought you'd—"

"Sorry." Gelsen picked up the telephone. "Yes. Certainly is a mess ... Have they? All right, I certainly will." He put down the telephone.

"Short and sweet," he told Macintyre. "We're to shut down temporarily."

"That won't be so easy," Macintyre said. "The watchbirds operate independent of any central control, you know. They come back once a week for a repair checkup. We'll have to turn them off then, one by one."

"Well, let's get to it. Monroe over on the Coast has shut down about a quarter of his birds."

"I think I can dope out a restricting circuit," Macintyre said.

"Fine," Gelsen replied bitterly. "You make me very happy."

The watchbirds were learning rapidly, expanding and adding to their knowledge. Loosely defined abstractions were extended, acted upon and re-extended.

To stop murder ...

Metal and electrons reason well, but not in a human fashion.

A living organism? Any living organism!

The watchbirds set themselves the task of protecting all living things.

The fly buzzed around the room, lighting on a table top, pausing a moment, then darting to a window sill.

The old man stalked it, a rolled newspaper in his hand.

Murderer!

The watchbirds swept down and saved the fly in the nick of time.

The old man writhed on the floor a minute and then was silent. He had been given only a mild shock, but it had been enough for his fluttery, cranky heart.

His victim had been saved, though, and this was the important thing. Save the victim and give the aggressor his just desserts.

Gelsen demanded angrily, "Why aren't they being turned off?"

The assistant control engineer gestured. In a corner of the repair room lay the senior control engineer. He was just regaining consciousness.

"He tried to turn one of them off," the assistant engineer said. Both his hands were knotted together. He was making a visible effort not to shake.

"That's ridiculous. They haven't got any sense of self-preservation."

"Then turn them off yourself. Besides, I don't think any more are going to come."

What could have happened? Gelsen began to piece it together. The watchbirds still hadn't decided on the limits of a living organism. When some of them were turned off in the Monroe plant, the rest must have correlated the data.

So they had been forced to assume that they were living organisms, as well.

No one had ever told them otherwise. Certainly they carried on most of the functions of living organisms.

Then the old fears hit him. Gelsen trembled and hurried out of the repair room. He wanted to find Macintyre in a hurry.

The nurse handed the surgeon the sponge.

"Scalpel."

She placed it in his hand. He started to make the first incision. And then he was aware of a disturbance.

"Who let that thing in?"

"I don't know," the nurse said, her voice muffled by the mask.

"Get it out of here."

The nurse waved her arms at the bright winged thing, but it fluttered over her head.

The surgeon proceeded with the incision—as long as he was able.

The watchbird drove him away and stood guard.

"Telephone the watchbird company!" the surgeon ordered. "Get them to turn the thing off."

The watchbird was preventing violence to a living organism.

The surgeon stood by helplessly while his patient died.

Fluttering high above the network of highways, the watchbird watched and waited. It had been constantly working for weeks now, without rest or repair. Rest and repair were impossible, because the watchbird couldn't allow itself—a living organism—to be murdered. And that was what happened when watchbirds returned to the factory.

There was a built-in order to return, after the lapse of a certain time period. But the watchbird had a stronger order to obey—preservation of life, including its own.

The definitions of murder were almost infinitely extended now, impossible to cope with. But the watchbird didn't consider that. It responded to its stimuli, whenever they came and whatever their source.

There was a new definition of living organism in its memory files. It had come as a result of the watchbird discovery that watchbirds were living organisms. And it had enormous ramifications.

The stimuli came! For the hundredth time that day, the bird wheeled and banked, dropping swiftly down to stop murder.

Jackson yawned and pulled his car to a shoulder of the road. He didn't notice the glittering dot in the sky. There was no reason for him to. Jackson wasn't contemplating murder, by any human definition.

This was a good spot for a nap, he decided. He had been driving for seven straight hours and his eyes were starting to fog. He reached out to turn off the ignition key—

And was knocked back against the side of the car.

"What in hell's wrong with you?" he asked indignantly. "All I want to do is—" He reached for the key again, and again he was smacked back.

Jackson knew better than to try a third time. He had been listening to the radio and he knew what the watchbirds did to stubborn violators.

"You mechanical jerk," he said to the waiting metal bird. "A car's not alive. I'm not trying to kill it."

But the watchbird only knew that a certain operation resulted in stopping an organism. The car was certainly a functioning organism. Wasn't it of metal, as were the watchbirds? Didn't it run?

Macintyre said, "Without repairs they'll run down." He shoved a pile of specification sheets out of his way.

"How soon?" Gelsen asked.

"Six months to a year. Say a year, barring accidents."

"A year," Gelsen said. "In the meantime, everything is stopping dead. Do you know the latest?"

"What?"

"The watchbirds have decided that the Earth is a living organism. They won't allow farmers to break ground for plowing. And, of course, everything else is a living organism—rabbits, beetles, flies, wolves, mosquitoes, lions, crocodiles, crows, and smaller forms of life such as bacteria."

"I know," Macintyre said.

"And you tell me they'll wear out in six months or a year. What happens now? What are we going to eat in six months?"

The engineer rubbed his chin. "We'll have to do something quick and fast. Ecological balance is gone to hell."

"Fast isn't the word. Instantaneously would be better." Gelsen lighted his thirty-fifth cigarette for the day. "At least I have the bitter satisfaction of saying, 'I told you so.' Although I'm just as responsible as the rest of the machine-worshipping fools."

Macintyre wasn't listening. He was thinking about watchbirds. "Like the rabbit plague in Australia."

"The death rate is mounting," Gelsen said. "Famine. Floods. Can't cut down trees. Doctors can't—what was that you said about Australia?"

"The rabbits," Macintyre repeated. "Hardly any left in Australia now."

"Why? How was it done?"

"Oh, found some kind of germ that attacked only rabbits. I think it was propagated by mosquitos—"

"Work on that," Gelsen said. "You might have something. I want you to get on the telephone, ask for an emergency hookup with the engineers of the other companies. Hurry it up. Together you may be able to dope out something."

"Right," Macintyre said. He grabbed a handful of blank paper and hurried to the telephone.

"What did I tell you?" Officer Celtrics said. He grinned at the captain. "Didn't I tell you scientists were nuts?"

"I didn't say you were wrong, did I?" the captain asked.

"No, but you weren't sure."

"Well, I'm sure now. You'd better get going. There's plenty of work for you."

"I know." Celtrics drew his revolver from its holster, checked it and put it back. "Are all the boys back, Captain?"

"All?" the captain laughed humorlessly. "Homicide has increased by fifty per cent. There's more murder now than there's ever been."

"Sure," Celtrics said. "The watchbirds are too busy guarding cars and slugging spiders." He started toward the door, then turned for a parting shot.

"Take my word, Captain. Machines are stupid."

The captain nodded.

Thousands of watchbirds, trying to stop countless millions of murders—a hopeless task. But the watchbirds didn't hope. Without consciousness, they experienced no sense of accomplishment, no fear of failure. Patiently they went about their jobs, obeying each stimulus as it came.

They couldn't be everywhere at the same time, but it wasn't necessary to be. People learned quickly what the watchbirds didn't like and refrained from doing it. It just wasn't safe. With their high speed and superfast senses, the watchbirds got around quickly.

And now they meant business. In their original directives there had been a provision made for killing a murderer, if all other means failed.

Why spare a murderer?

It backfired. The watchbirds extracted the fact that murder and crimes of violence had increased geometrically since they had begun operation. This was true, because their new definitions increased the possibilities of murder. But to the watchbirds, the rise showed that the first methods had failed.

Simple logic. If A doesn't work, try B. The watchbirds shocked to kill.

Slaughterhouses in Chicago stopped and cattle starved to death in their pens, because farmers in the Midwest couldn't cut hay or harvest grain.

No one had told the watchbirds that all life depends on carefully balanced murders.

Starvation didn't concern the watchbirds, since it was an act of omission.

Their interest lay only in acts of commission.

Hunters sat home, glaring at the silver dots in the sky, longing to shoot them down. But for the most part, they didn't try. The watchbirds were quick to sense the murder intent and to punish it.

Fishing boats swung idle at their moorings in San Pedro and Glouces- ter. Fish were living organisms.

Farmers cursed and spat and died, trying to harvest the crop. Grain was alive and thus worthy of protection. Potatoes were as important to the watchbird as any other living organism. The death of a blade of grass was equal to the assassination of a President—

To the watchbirds.

And, of course, certain machines were living. This followed, since the watchbirds were machines and living.

God help you if you maltreated your radio. Turning it off meant killing it. Obviously—its voice was silenced, the red glow of its tubes faded, it grew cold.

The watchbirds tried to guard their other charges. Wolves were slaugh- tered, trying to kill rabbits. Rabbits were electrocuted, trying to eat veg- etables. Creepers were burned out in the act of strangling trees.

A butterfly was executed, caught in the act of outraging a rose.

This control was spasmodic, because of the fewness of the watchbirds. A billion watchbirds couldn't have carried out the ambitious project set by the thousands.

The effect was of a murderous force, ten thousand bolts of irrational lightning raging around the country, striking a thousand times a day.

Lightning which anticipated your moves and punished your intentions.

"Gentlemen, please," the government representative begged. "We must hurry."

The seven manufacturers stopped talking.

"Before we begin this meeting formally," the president of Monroe said, "I want to say something. We do not feel ourselves responsible for this unhappy state of affairs. It was a government project; the government must accept the responsibility, both moral and financial."

Gelsen shrugged his shoulders. It was hard to believe that these men, just a few weeks ago, had been willing to accept the glory of saving the world. Now they wanted to shrug off the responsibility when the salvation went amiss.

"I'm positive that that need not concern us now," the representative as- sured him. "We must hurry. You engineers have done an excellent job. I am proud of the cooperation you have shown in this emergency. You are hereby empowered to put the outlined plan into action."

"Wait a minute," Gelsen said.

"There is no time."

"The plan's no good."

"Don't you think it will work?"

"Of course it will work. But I'm afraid the cure will be worse than the disease."

The manufacturers looked as though they would have enjoyed throttling Gelsen. He didn't hesitate.

"Haven't we learned yet?" he asked. "Don't you see that you can't cure human problems by mechanization?"

"Mr. Gelsen," the president of Monroe said, "I would enjoy hearing you philosophize, but, unfortunately, people are being killed. Crops are being ruined. There is famine in some sections of the country already. The watchbirds must be stopped at once!"

"Murder must be stopped, too. I remember all of us agreeing upon that. But this is not the way!"

"What would you suggest?" the representative asked.

Gelsen took a deep breath. What he was about to say took all the courage he had.

"Let the watchbirds run down by themselves," Gelsen suggested.

There was a near-riot. The government representative broke it up.

"Let's take our lesson," Gelsen urged, "admit that we were wrong trying to cure human problems by mechanical means. Start again. Use machines, yes, but not as judges and teachers and fathers."

"Ridiculous," the representative said coldly. "Mr. Gelsen, you are overwrought. I suggest you control yourself." He cleared his throat. "All of you are ordered by the President to carry out the plan you have submitted." He looked sharply at Gelsen. "Not to do so will be treason."

"I'll cooperate to the best of my ability," Gelsen said.

"Good. Those assembly lines must be rolling within the week."

Gelsen walked out of the room alone. Now he was confused again. Had he been right or was he just another visionary? Certainly, he hadn't explained himself with much clarity.

Did he know what he meant?

Gelsen cursed under his breath. He wondered why he couldn't ever be sure of anything. Weren't there any values he could hold on to?

He hurried to the airport and to his plant.

The watchbird was operating erratically now. Many of its delicate parts were out of line, worn by almost continuous operation. But gallantly it responded when the stimuli came.

A spider was attacking a fly. The watchbird swooped down to the rescue.

Simultaneously, it became aware of something overhead. The watchbird wheeled to meet it.

There was a sharp crackle and a power bolt whizzed by the watchbird's wing. Angrily, it spat a shock wave.

The attacker was heavily insulated. Again it spat at the watchbird. This time, a bolt smashed through a wing, the watchbird darted away, but the attacker went after it in a burst of speed, throwing out more crackling power.

The watchbird fell, but managed to send out its message. Urgent! A new menace to living organisms and this was the deadliest yet!

Other watchbirds around the country integrated the message. Their thinking centers searched for an answer.

"Well, Chief, they bagged fifty today," Macintyre said, coming into Gelsen's office.

"Fine," Gelsen said, not looking at the engineer.

"Not so fine." Macintyre sat down. "Lord, I'm tired! It was seventy-two yesterday."

"I know." On Gelsen's desk were several dozen lawsuits, which he was sending to the government with a prayer.

"They'll pick up again, though," Macintyre said confidently. "The Hawks are especially built to hunt down watchbirds. They're stronger, faster, and they've got better armor. We really rolled them out in a hurry, huh?"

"We sure did."

"The watchbirds are pretty good, too," Macintyre had to admit. "They're learning to take cover. They're trying a lot of stunts. You know, each one that goes down tells the others something."

Gelsen didn't answer.

"But anything the watchbirds can do, the Hawks can do better," Macintyre said cheerfully. "The Hawks have special learning circuits for hunting. They're more flexible than the watchbirds. They learn faster."

Gelsen gloomily stood up, stretched, and walked to the window. The sky was blank. Looking out, he realized that his uncertainties were over. Right or wrong, he had made up his mind.

"Tell me," he said, still watching the sky, "what will the Hawks hunt after they get all the watchbirds?"

"Huh?" Macintyre said. "Why—"

"Just to be on the safe side, you'd better design something to hunt down the Hawks. Just in case, I mean."

"You think—"

"All I know is that the Hawks are self-controlled. So were the watchbirds. Remote control would have been too slow, the argument went on. The idea was to get the watchbirds and get them fast. That meant no restricting circuits."

"We can dope something out," Macintyre said uncertainly.

"You've got an aggressive machine up in the air now. A murder machine. Before that it was an anti-murder machine. Your next gadget will have to be even more self-sufficient, won't it?"

Macintyre didn't answer.

"I don't hold you responsible," Gelsen said. "It's me. It's everyone."

In the air outside was a swift-moving dot.

"That's what comes," said Gelsen, "of giving a machine the job that was our own responsibility."

Overhead, a Hawk was zeroing in on a watchbird.

The armored murder machine had learned a lot in a few days. Its sole function was to kill. At present it was impelled toward a certain type of living organism, metallic like itself.

But the Hawk had just discovered that there were other types of living organisms, too—

Which had to be murdered.

Bad Medicine

On May 2, 2103, Elwood Caswell walked rapidly down Broadway with a loaded revolver hidden in his coat pocket. He didn't want to use the weapon, but feared he might anyhow. This was a justifiable assumption, for Caswell was a homicidal maniac.

It was a gentle, misty spring day and the air held the smell of rain and blossoming-dogwood. Caswell gripped the revolver in his sweaty right hand and tried to think of a single valid reason why he should not kill a man named Magnessen, who, the other day, had commented on how well Caswell looked.

What business was it of Magnessen's how he looked? Damned busybodies, always spoiling things for everybody....

Caswell was a choleric little man with fierce red eyes, bulldog jowls and ginger-red hair. He was the sort you would expect to find perched on a detergent box, orating to a crowd of lunching businessmen and amused students, shouting, "Mars for the Martians, Venus for the Venusians!"

But in truth, Caswell was uninterested in the deplorable social conditions of extraterrestrials. He was a jetbus conductor for the New York Rapid Transit Corporation. He minded his own business. And he was quite mad.

Fortunately, he knew this at least part of the time, with at least half of his mind.

Perspiring freely, Caswell continued down Broadway toward the 43rd Street branch of Home Therapy Appliances, Inc. His friend Magnessen would be finishing work soon, returning to his little apartment less than a block from Caswell's. How easy it would be, how pleasant, to saunter in, exchange a few words and....

No! Caswell took a deep gulp of air and reminded himself that he didn't really want to kill anyone. It was not right to kill people. The authorities would lock him up, his friends wouldn't understand, his mother would never have approved.

But these arguments seemed pallid, over-intellectual and entirely without force. The simple fact remained--he wanted to kill Magnessen.

Could so strong a desire be wrong? Or even unhealthy?

Yes, it could! With an agonized groan, Caswell sprinted the last few steps into the Home Therapy Appliances Store.

Just being within such a place gave him an immediate sense of relief. The lighting was discreet, the draperies were neutral, the displays of glittering therapy machines were neither too bland nor obstreperous. It was the kind of place where a man could happily lie down on the carpet in the shadow of the therapy machines, secure in the knowledge that help for any sort of trouble was at hand.

A clerk with fair hair and a long, supercilious nose glided up softly, but not too softly, and murmured, "May one help?"

"Therapy!" said Caswell.

"Of course, sir," the clerk answered, smoothing his lapels and smiling winningly. "That is what we are here for." He gave Caswell a searching look, performed an instant mental diagnosis, and tapped a gleaming white-and-copper machine.

"Now this," the clerk said, "is the new Alcoholic Reliever, built by IBM and advertised in the leading magazines. A handsome piece of furniture, I think you will agree, and not out of place in any home. It opens into a television set."

With a flick of his narrow wrist, the clerk opened the Alcoholic Reliever, revealing a 52-inch screen.

"I need--" Caswell began.

"Therapy," the clerk finished for him. "Of course. I just wanted to point out that this model need never cause embarrassment for yourself, your friends or loved ones. Notice, if you will, the recessed dial which controls the desired degree of drinking. See? If you do not wish total abstinence, you can set it to heavy, moderate, social or light. That is a new feature, unique in mechanotherapy."

"I am not an alcoholic," Caswell said, with considerable dignity. "The New York Rapid Transit Corporation does not hire alcoholics."

"Oh," said the clerk, glancing distrustfully at Caswell's bloodshot eyes. "You seem a little nervous. Perhaps the portable Bendix Anxiety Reducer--"

"Anxiety's not my ticket, either. What have you got for homicidal mania?"

The clerk pursed his lips. "Schizophrenic or manic-depressive origins?"

"I don't know," Caswell admitted, somewhat taken aback.

"It really doesn't matter," the clerk told him. "Just a private theory of my own. From my experience in the store, redheads and blonds are prone to schizophrenia, while brunettes incline toward the manic-depressive."

"That's interesting. Have you worked here long?"

"A week. Now then, here is just what you need, sir." He put his hand affectionately on a squat black machine with chrome trim.

"What's that?"

"That, sir, is the Rex Regenerator, built by General Motors. Isn't it handsome? It can go with any decor and opens up into a well-stocked bar. Your friends, family, loved ones need never know--"

"Will it cure a homicidal urge?" Caswell asked. "A strong one?"

"Absolutely. Don't confuse this with the little ten amp neurosis models. This is a hefty, heavy-duty, twenty-five amp machine for a really deep-rooted major condition."

"That's what I've got," said Caswell, with pardonable pride.

"This baby'll jolt it out of you. Big, heavy-duty thrust bearings! Oversize heat absorbers! Completely insulated! Sensitivity range of over--"

"I'll take it," Caswell said. "Right now. I'll pay cash."

"Fine! I'll just telephone Storage and--"

"This one'll do," Caswell said, pulling out his billfold. "I'm in a hurry to use it. I want to kill my friend Magnessen, you know."

The clerk clucked sympathetically. "You wouldn't want to do that ... Plus five percent sales tax. Thank you, sir. Full instructions are inside."

Caswell thanked him, lifted the Regenerator in both arms and hurried out.

After figuring his commission, the clerk smiled to himself and lighted a cigarette. His enjoyment was spoiled when the manager, a large man impressively equipped with pince-nez, marched out of his office.

"Haskins," the manager said, "I thought I asked you to rid yourself of that filthy habit."

"Yes, Mr. Follansby, sorry, sir," Haskins apologized, snubbing out the cigarette. "I'll use the display Denicotinizer at once. Made rather a good sale, Mr. Follansby. One of the big Rex Regenerators."

"Really?" said the manager, impressed. "It isn't often we--wait a minute! You didn't sell the floor model, did you?"

"Why--why, I'm afraid I did, Mr. Follansby. The customer was in such a terrible hurry. Was there any reason--"

Mr. Follansby gripped his prominent white forehead in both hands, as though he wished to rip it off. "Haskins, I told you. I must have told you! That display Regenerator was a Martian model. For giving mechanotherapy to Martians."

"Oh," Haskins said. He thought for a moment. "Oh."

Mr. Follansby stared at his clerk in grim silence.

"But does it really matter?" Haskins asked quickly. "Surely the machine won't discriminate. I should think it would treat a homicidal tendency even if the patient were not a Martian."

"The Martian race has never had the slightest tendency toward homicide. A Martian Regenerator doesn't even process the concept. Of course the Regenerator will treat him. It has to. But what will it treat?"

"Oh," said Haskins.

"That poor devil must be stopped before--you say he was homicidal? I don't know what will happen! Quick, what is his address?"

"Well, Mr. Follansby, he was in such a terrible hurry--"

The manager gave him a long, unbelieving look. "Get the police! Call the General Motors Security Division! Find him!"

Haskins raced for the door.

"Wait!" yelled the manager, struggling into a raincoat. "I'm coming, too."

Elwood Caswell returned to his apartment by taxicopter. He lugged the

Regenerator into his living room, put it down near the couch and studied it thoughtfully.

"That clerk was right," he said after a while. "It does go with the room."

Esthetically, the Regenerator was a success.

Caswell admired it for a few more moments, then went into the kitchen and fixed himself a chicken sandwich. He ate slowly, staring fixedly at a point just above and to the left of his kitchen clock.

Damn you, Magnessen! Dirty no-good lying shifty-eyed enemy of all that's decent and clean in the world....

Taking the revolver from his pocket, he laid it on the table. With a stiffened forefinger, he poked it into different positions.

It was time to begin therapy.

Except that....

Caswell realized worriedly that he didn't want to lose the desire to kill Magnessen. What would become of him if he lost that urge? His life would lose all purpose, all coherence, all flavor and zest. It would be quite dull, really.

Moreover, he had a great and genuine grievance against Magnessen, one he didn't like to think about.

Irene!

His poor sister, debauched by the subtle and insidious Magnessen, ruined by him and cast aside. What better reason could a man have to take his revolver and....

Caswell finally remembered that he did not have a sister.

Now was really the time to begin therapy.

He went into the living room and found the operating instructions tucked into a ventilation louver of the machine. He opened them and read:

To Operate All Rex Model Regenerators:

1. Place the Regenerator near a comfortable couch. (A comfortable couch can be purchased as an additional accessory from any General Motors dealer.)

2. Plug in the machine.

3. Affix the adjustable contact-band to the forehead.

And that's all! Your Regenerator will do the rest! There will be no language bar or dialect problem, since the Regenerator communicates by Direct Sense Contact (Patent Pending). All you must do is cooperate.

Try not to feel any embarrassment or shame. Everyone has problems and many are worse than yours! Your Regenerator has no interest in your morals or ethical standards, so don't feel it is 'judging' you. It desires only to aid you in becoming well and happy.

As soon as it has collected and processed enough data, your Regenerator will begin treatment. You make the sessions as short or as long as you like. You are the boss! And of course you can end a session at any time.

That's all there is to it! Simple, isn't it? Now plug in your General Motors Regenerator and GET SANE!

"Nothing hard about that," Caswell said to himself. He pushed the Regenerator closer to the couch and plugged it in. He lifted the headband, started to slip it on, stopped.

"I feel so silly!" he giggled.

Abruptly he closed his mouth and stared pugnaciously at the black-and-chrome machine.

"So you think you can make me sane, huh?"

The Regenerator didn't answer.

"Oh, well, go ahead and try." He slipped the headband over his forehead, crossed his arms on his chest and leaned back.

Nothing happened. Caswell settled himself more comfortably on the couch. He scratched his shoulder and put the headband at a more comfortable angle. Still nothing. His thoughts began to wander.

Magnessen! You noisy, overbearing oaf, you disgusting--

"Good afternoon," a voice murmured in his head. "I am your mechanotherapist."

Caswell twitched guiltily. "Hello. I was just--you know, just sort of--"

"Of course," the machine said soothingly. "Don't we all? I am now scanning the material in your preconscious with the intent of synthesis, diagnosis, prognosis, and treatment. I find...."

"Yes?"

"Just one moment." The Regenerator was silent for several minutes. Then, hesitantly, it said, "This is beyond doubt a most unusual case."

"Really?" Caswell asked, pleased.

"Yes. The coefficients seem--I'm not sure...." The machine's robotic voice grew feeble. The pilot light began to flicker and fade.

"Hey, what's the matter?"

"Confusion," said the machine. "Of course," it went on in a stronger voice, "the unusual nature of the symptoms need not prove entirely baffling to a competent therapeutic machine. A symptom, no matter how bizarre, is no more than a signpost, an indication of inner difficulty. And all symptoms can be related to the broad mainstream of proven theory. Since the theory is effective, the symptoms must relate. We will proceed on that assumption."

"Are you sure you know what you're doing?" asked Caswell, feeling lightheaded.

The machine snapped back, its pilot light blazing. "Mechanotherapy today is an exact science and admits no significant errors. We will proceed with a word-association test."

"Fire away," said Caswell.

"House?"

"Home."

"Dog?"

"Cat."

"Fleefl?"

Caswell hesitated, trying to figure out the word. It sounded vaguely Martian, but it might be Venusian or even--

"Fleefl?" the Regenerator repeated.

"Marfoosh," Caswell replied, making up the word on the spur of the moment.

"Loud?"

"Sweet."

"Green?"

"Mother."

"Thanagoyes?"

"Patamathonga."

"Arrides?"

"Nexothesmodrastica."

"Chtheesnohelgnopteces?"

"Rigamaroo latasentricpropatria!" Caswell shot back. It was a collection of sounds he was particularly proud of. The average man would not have been able to pronounce them.

"Hmm," said the Regenerator. "The pattern fits. It always does."

"What pattern?"

"You have," the machine informed him, "a classic case of feem desire, complicated by strong dwarkish intentions."

"I do? I thought I was homicidal."

"That term has no referent," the machine said severely. "Therefore I must reject it as nonsense syllabification. Now consider these points: The feem desire is perfectly normal. Never forget that. But it is usually replaced at an early age by the hovendish revulsion. Individuals lacking in this basic environmental response--"

"I'm not absolutely sure I know what you're talking about," Caswell confessed.

"Please, sir! We must establish one thing at once. You are the patient. I am the mechanotherapist. You have brought your troubles to me for treatment. But you cannot expect help unless you cooperate."

"All right," Caswell said. "I'll try."

Up to now, he had been bathed in a warm glow of superiority. Everything the machine said had seemed mildly humorous. As a matter of fact, he had felt capable of pointing out a few things wrong with the mechanotherapist.

Now that sense of well-being evaporated, as it always did, and Caswell was alone, terribly alone and lost, a creature of his compulsions, in search of a little peace and contentment.

He would undergo anything to find them. Sternly he reminded himself that he had no right to comment on the mechanotherapist. These machines knew what they were doing and had been doing it for a long time. He would cooperate, no matter how outlandish the treatment seemed from his layman's viewpoint.

But it was obvious, Caswell thought, settling himself grimly on the couch, that mechanotherapy was going to be far more difficult than he had imagined.

The search for the missing customer had been brief and useless. He was nowhere to be found on the teeming New York streets and no one could remember seeing a red-haired, red-eyed little man lugging a black therapeutic machine.

It was all too common a sight.

In answer to an urgent telephone call, the police came immediately, four of them, led by a harassed young lieutenant of detectives named Smith.

Smith just had time to ask, "Say, why don't you people put tags on things?" when there was an interruption.

A man pushed his way past the policeman at the door. He was tall and gnarled and ugly, and his eyes were deep-set and bleakly blue. His clothes, unpressed and uncaring, hung on him like corrugated iron.

"What do you want?" Lieutenant Smith asked.

The ugly man flipped back his lapel, showing a small silver badge beneath. "I'm John Rath, General Motors Security Division."

"Oh ... Sorry, sir," Lieutenant Smith said, saluting. "I didn't think you people would move in so fast."

Rath made a noncommittal noise. "Have you checked for prints, Lieutenant? The customer might have touched some other therapy machine."

"I'll get right on it, sir," Smith said. It wasn't often that one of the operatives from GM, GE, or IBM came down to take a personal hand. If a local cop showed he was really clicking, there just might be the possibility of an Industrial Transfer....

Rath turned to Follansby and Haskins, and transfixed them with a gaze as piercing and as impersonal as a radar beam. "Let's have the full story," he said, taking a notebook and pencil from a shapeless pocket.

He listened to the tale in ominous silence. Finally he closed his notebook, thrust it back into his pocket and said, "The therapeutic machines are a sacred trust. To give a customer the wrong machine is a betrayal of that trust, a violation of the Public Interest, and a defamation of the Company's good reputation."

The manager nodded in agreement, glaring at his unhappy clerk.

"A Martian model," Rath continued, "should never have been on the floor in the first place."

"I can explain that," Follansby said hastily. "We needed a demonstrator model and I wrote to the Company, telling them--"

"This might," Rath broke in inexorably, "be considered a case of gross criminal negligence."

Both the manager and the clerk exchanged horrified looks. They were thinking of the General Motors Reformatory outside of Detroit, where Company offenders passed their days in sullen silence, monotonously drawing microcircuits for pocket television sets.

"However, that is out of my jurisdiction," Rath said. He turned his baleful gaze full upon Haskins. "You are certain that the customer never mentioned his name?"

"No, sir. I mean yes, I'm sure," Haskins replied rattledly.

"Did he mention any names at all?"

Haskins plunged his face into his hands. He looked up and said eagerly, "Yes! He wanted to kill someone! A friend of his!"

"Who?" Rath asked, with terrible patience.

"The friend's name was--let me think--Magneton! That was it! Magneton! Or was it Morrison? Oh, dear...."

Mr. Rath's iron face registered a rather corrugated disgust. People were useless as witnesses. Worse than useless, since they were frequently misleading. For reliability, give him a robot every time.

"Didn't he mention anything significant?"

"Let me think!" Haskins said, his face twisting into a fit of concentration.

Rath waited.

Mr. Follansby cleared his throat. "I was just thinking, Mr. Rath. About that Martian machine. It won't treat a Terran homicidal case as homicidal, will it?"

"Of course not. Homicide is unknown on Mars."

"Yes. But what will it do? Might it not reject the entire case as unsuitable? Then the customer would merely return the Regenerator with a complaint and we would--"

Mr. Rath shook his head. "The Rex Regenerator must treat if it finds evidence of psychosis. By Martian standards, the customer is a very sick man, a psychotic--no matter what is wrong with him."

Follansby removed his pince-nez and polished them rapidly. "What will the machine do, then?"

"It will treat him for the Martian illness most analogous to his case. Feem desire, I should imagine, with various complications. As for what will happen once treatment begins, I don't know. I doubt whether anyone knows, since it has never happened before. Offhand, I would say there are two major alternatives: the patient may reject the therapy out of hand, in which case he is left with his homicidal mania unabated. Or he may accept the Martian therapy and reach a cure."

Mr. Follansby's face brightened. "Ah! A cure is possible!"

"You don't understand," Rath said. "He may effect a cure of his nonexistent Martian psychosis. But to cure something that is not there is, in effect, to erect a gratuitous delusional system. You might say that the machine would work in reverse, producing psychosis instead of removing it."

Mr. Follansby groaned and leaned against a Bell Psychosomatica.

"The result," Rath summed up, "would be to convince the customer that he was a Martian. A sane Martian, naturally."

Haskins suddenly shouted, "I remember! I remember now! He said he worked for the New York Rapid Transit Corporation! I remember distinctly!"

"That's a break," Rath said, reaching for the telephone.

Haskins wiped his perspiring face in relief. "And I just remembered something else that should make it easier still."

"What?"

"The customer said he had been an alcoholic at one time. I'm sure of it, because he was interested at first in the IBM Alcoholic Reliever, until I talked him out of it. He had red hair, you know, and I've had a theory for some time about red-headedness and alcoholism. It seems--"

"Excellent," Rath said. "Alcoholism will be on his records. It narrows the search considerably."

As he dialed the NYRT Corporation, the expression on his craglike face was almost pleasant.

It was good, for a change, to find that a human could retain some significant facts.

"But surely you remember your goricae?" the Regenerator was saying.

"No," Caswell answered wearily.

"Tell me, then, about your juvenile experiences with the thorastrian fleep."

"Never had any."

"Hmm. Blockage," muttered the machine. "Resentment. Repression. Are you sure you don't remember your goricae and what it meant to you? The experience is universal."

"Not for me," Caswell said, swallowing a yawn.

He had been undergoing mechanotherapy for close to four hours and it struck him as futile. For a while, he had talked voluntarily about his childhood, his mother and father, his older brother. But the Regenerator had asked him to put aside those fantasies. The patient's relationships to an imaginary parent or sibling, it explained, were unworkable and of minor importance psychologically. The important thing was the patient's feelings--both revealed and repressed--toward his goricae.

"Aw, look," Caswell complained, "I don't even know what a goricae is."

"Of course you do. You just won't let yourself know."

"I don't know. Tell me."

"It would be better if you told me."

"How can I?" Caswell raged. "I don't know!"

"What do you imagine a goricae would be?"

"A forest fire," Caswell said. "A salt tablet. A jar of denatured alcohol. A small screwdriver. Am I getting warm? A notebook. A revolver--"

"These associations are meaningful," the Regenerator assured him.

"Your attempt at randomness shows a clearly underlying pattern. Do you begin to recognize it?"

"What in hell is a goricae?" Caswell roared.

"The tree that nourished you during infancy, and well into puberty, if my theory about you is correct. Inadvertently, the goricae stifled your necessary rejection of the feem desire. This in turn gave rise to your present urge to dwark someone in a vlendish manner."

"No tree nourished me."

"You cannot recall the experience?"

"Of course not. It never happened."

"You are sure of that?"

"Positive."

"Not even the tiniest bit of doubt?"

"No! No goricae ever nourished me. Look, I can break off these sessions at any time, right?"

"Of course," the Regenerator said. "But it would not be advisable at this moment. You are expressing anger, resentment, fear. By your rigidly summary rejection--"

"Nuts," said Caswell, and pulled off the headband.

The silence was wonderful. Caswell stood up, yawned, stretched and massaged the back of his neck. He stood in front of the humming black machine and gave it a long leer.

"You couldn't cure me of a common cold," he told it.

Stiffly he walked the length of the living room and returned to the Regenerator.

"Lousy fake!" he shouted.

Caswell went into the kitchen and opened a bottle of beer. His revolver was still on the table, gleaming dully.

Magnessen! You unspeakable treacherous filth! You fiend incarnate! You inhuman, hideous monster! Someone must destroy you, Magnessen! Someone....

Someone? He himself would have to do it. Only he knew the bottomless depths of Magnessen's depravity, his viciousness, his disgusting lust for power.

Yes, it was his duty, Caswell thought. But strangely, the knowledge brought him no pleasure.

After all, Magnessen was his friend.

He stood up, ready for action. He tucked the revolver into his right-hand coat pocket and glanced at the kitchen clock. Nearly six-thirty. Magnessen would be home now, gulping his dinner, grinning over his plans.

This was the perfect time to take him.

Caswell strode to the door, opened it, started through, and stopped.

A thought had crossed his mind, a thought so tremendously involved, so meaningful, so far-reaching in its implications that he was stirred to his depths. Caswell tried desperately to shake off the knowledge it brought. But the thought, permanently etched upon his memory, would not depart.

Under the circumstances, he could do only one thing.

He returned to the living room, sat down on the couch and slipped on the headband.

The Regenerator said, "Yes?"

"It's the damnedest thing," Caswell said, "but do you know, I think I do remember my goricae!"

John Rath contacted the New York Rapid Transit Corporation by tele-video and was put into immediate contact with Mr. Bemis, a plump, tanned man with watchful eyes.

"Alcoholism?" Mr. Bemis repeated, after the problem was explained. Unobtrusively, he turned on his tape recorder. "Among our employees?" Pressing a button beneath his foot, Bemis alerted Transit Security, Publicity, Intercompany Relations, and the Psychoanalysis Division. This done, he looked earnestly at Rath. "Not a chance of it, my dear sir. Just between us, why does General Motors really want to know?"

Rath smiled bitterly. He should have anticipated this. NYRT and GM had had their differences in the past. Officially, there was cooperation between the two giant corporations. But for all practical purposes--

"The question is in terms of the Public Interest," Rath said.

"Oh, certainly," Mr. Bemis replied, with a subtle smile. Glancing at his tattle board, he noticed that several company executives had tapped in on his line. This might mean a promotion, if handled properly.

"The Public Interest of GM," Mr. Bemis added with polite nastiness. "The insinuation is, I suppose, that drunken conductors are operating our jetbuses and helis?"

"Of course not. I was searching for a single alcoholic predilection, an individual latency--"

"There's no possibility of it. We at Rapid Transit do not hire people with even the merest tendency in that direction. And may I suggest, sir, that you clean your own house before making implications about others?"

And with that, Mr. Bemis broke the connection.

No one was going to put anything over on him.

"Dead end," Rath said heavily. He turned and shouted, "Smith! Did you find any prints?"

Lieutenant Smith, his coat off and sleeves rolled up, bounded over. "Nothing usable, sir."

Rath's thin lips tightened. It had been close to seven hours since the customer had taken the Martian machine. There was no telling what harm had been done by now. The customer would be justified in bringing suit against the Company. Not that the money mattered much; it was the bad publicity that was to be avoided at all costs.

"Beg pardon, sir," Haskins said.

Rath ignored him. What next? Rapid Transit was not going to cooperate. Would the Armed Services make their records available for scansion by somatotype and pigmentation?

"Sir," Haskins said again.

"What is it?"

"I just remembered the customer's friend's name. It was Magnessen."

"Are you sure of that?"

"Absolutely," Haskins said, with the first confidence he had shown in hours. "I've taken the liberty of looking him up in the telephone book, sir. There's only one Manhattan listing under that name."

Rath glowered at him from under shaggy eyebrows. "Haskins, I hope you are not wrong about this. I sincerely hope that."

"I do too, sir," Haskins admitted, feeling his knees begin to shake.

"Because if you are," Rath said, "I will ... Never mind. Let's go!"

By police escort, they arrived at the address in fifteen minutes. It was an ancient brownstone and Magnessen's name was on a second-floor door. They knocked.

The door opened and a stocky, crop-headed, shirt-sleeved man in his thirties stood before them. He turned slightly pale at the sight of so many uniforms, but held his ground.

"What is this?" he demanded.

"You Magnessen?" Lieutenant Smith barked.

"Yeah. What's the beef? If it's about my hi-fi playing too loud, I can tell you that old hag downstairs--"

"May we come in?" Rath asked. "It's important."

Magnessen seemed about to refuse, so Rath pushed past him, followed by Smith, Follansby, Haskins, and a small army of policemen. Magnessen turned to face them, bewildered, defiant and more than a little awed.

"Mr. Magnessen," Rath said, in the pleasantest voice he could muster, "I hope you'll forgive the intrusion. Let me assure you, it is in the Public Interest, as well as your own. Do you know a short, angry-looking, red-haired, red-eyed man?"

"Yes," Magnessen said slowly and warily.

Haskins let out a sigh of relief.

"Would you tell us his name and address?" asked Rath.

"I suppose you mean--hold it! What's he done?"

"Nothing."

"Then what you want him for?"

"There's no time for explanations," Rath said. "Believe me, it's in his own best interest, too. What is his name?"

Magnessen studied Rath's ugly, honest face, trying to make up his mind.

Lieutenant Smith said, "Come on, talk, Magnessen, if you know what's good for you. We want the name and we want it quick."

It was the wrong approach. Magnessen lit a cigarette, blew smoke in Smith's direction and inquired, "You got a warrant, buddy?"

"You bet I have," Smith said, striding forward. "I'll warrant you, wise guy."

"Stop it!" Rath ordered. "Lieutenant Smith, thank you for your assistance. I won't need you any longer."

Smith left sulkily, taking his platoon with him.

Rath said, "I apologize for Smith's over-eagerness. You had better hear the problem." Briefly but fully, he told the story of the customer and the Martian therapeutic machine.

When he was finished, Magnessen looked more suspicious than ever. "You say he wants to kill me?"

"Definitely."

"That's a lie! I don't know what your game is, mister, but you'll never make me believe that. Elwood's my best friend. We been best friends since we was kids. We been in service together. Elwood would cut off his arm for me. And I'd do the same for him."

"Yes, yes," Rath said impatiently, "in a sane frame of mind, he would. But your friend Elwood--is that his first name or last?"

"First," Magnessen said tauntingly.

"Your friend Elwood is psychotic."

"You don't know him. That guy loves me like a brother. Look, what's Elwood really done? Defaulted on some payments or something? I can help out."

"You thickheaded imbecile!" Rath shouted. "I'm trying to save your life, and the life and sanity of your friend!"

"But how do I know?" Magnessen pleaded. "You guys come busting in here--"

"You can trust me," Rath said.

Magnessen studied Rath's face and nodded sourly. "His name's Elwood Caswell. He lives just down the block at number 341."

The man who came to the door was short, with red hair and red-rimmed eyes. His right hand was thrust into his coat pocket. He seemed very calm.

"Are you Elwood Caswell?" Rath asked. "The Elwood Caswell who bought a Regenerator early this afternoon at the Home Therapy Appliances Store?"

"Yes," said Caswell. "Won't you come in?"

Inside Caswell's small living room, they saw the Regenerator, glistening black and chrome, standing near the couch. It was unplugged.

"Have you used it?" Rath asked anxiously.

"Yes."

Follansby stepped forward. "Mr. Caswell, I don't know how to explain this, but we made a terrible mistake. The Regenerator you took was a Martian model--for giving therapy to Martians."

"I know," said Caswell.

"You do?"

"Of course. It became pretty obvious after a while."

"It was a dangerous situation," Rath said. "Especially for a man with your--ah--troubles." He studied Caswell covertly. The man seemed fine, but appearances were frequently deceiving, especially with psychotics. Caswell had been homicidal; there was no reason why he should not still be.

And Rath began to wish he had not dismissed Smith and his policemen so summarily. Sometimes an armed squad was a comforting thing to have around.

Caswell walked across the room to the therapeutic machine. One hand was still in his jacket pocket; the other he laid affectionately upon the Regenerator.

"The poor thing tried its best," he said. "Of course, it couldn't cure what wasn't there." He laughed. "But it came very near succeeding!"

Rath studied Caswell's face and said, in a trained, casual tone, "Glad there was no harm, sir. The Company will, of course, reimburse you for your lost time and for your mental anguish--"

"Naturally," Caswell said.

"--and we will substitute a proper Terran Regenerator at once."

"That won't be necessary."

"It won't?"

"No." Caswell's voice was decisive. "The machine's attempt at therapy forced me into a compete self-appraisal. There was a moment of absolute insight, during which I was able to evaluate and discard my homicidal intentions toward poor Magnessen."

Rath nodded dubiously. "You feel no such urge now?"

"Not in the slightest."

Rath frowned deeply, started to say something, and stopped. He turned to Follansby and Haskins. "Get that machine out of here. I'll have a few things to say to you at the store."

The manager and the clerk lifted the Regenerator and left.

Rath took a deep breath. "Mr. Caswell, I would strongly advise that you accept a new Regenerator from the Company, gratis. Unless a cure is effected in a proper mechanotherapeutic manner, there is always the danger of a setback."

"No danger with me," Caswell said, airily but with deep conviction. "Thank you for your consideration, sir. And good night."

Rath shrugged and walked to the door.

"Wait!" Caswell called.

Rath turned. Caswell had taken his hand out of his pocket. In it was a revolver. Rath felt sweat trickle down his arms. He calculated the distance between himself and Caswell. Too far.

"Here," Caswell said, extending the revolver butt-first. "I won't need this any longer."

Rath managed to keep his face expressionless as he accepted the revolver and stuck it into a shapeless pocket.

"Good night," Caswell said. He closed the door behind Rath and bolted it.

At last he was alone.

Caswell walked into the kitchen. He opened a bottle of beer, took a deep swallow and sat down at the kitchen table. He stared fixedly at a point just above and to the left of the clock.

He had to form his plans now. There was no time to lose.

Magnessen! That inhuman monster who cut down the Caswell goricae! Magnessen! The man who, even now, was secretly planning to infect New York with the abhorrent feem desire! Oh, Magnessen, I wish you a long, long life, filled with the torture I can inflict on you. And to start with....

Caswell smiled to himself as he planned exactly how he would dwark Magnessen in a vlendish manner.

FOREVER

Illustrated by DICK FRANCIS

Of all the irksome, frustrating, maddening discoveries—was there no way of keeping it discovered?

With so much at stake, Charles Dennison should not have been careless. An inventor cannot afford carelessness, particularly when his invention is extremely valuable and obviously patentable. There are too many grasping hands ready to seize what belongs to someone else, too many men who feast upon the creativity of the innocent.

A touch of paranoia would have served Dennison well; but he was lacking in that vital characteristic of inventors. And he didn't even realize the full extent of his carelessness until a bullet, fired from a silenced weapon, chipped a granite wall not three inches from his head.

Then he knew. But by then it was too late.

Charles Dennison had been left a more than adequate income by his father. He had gone to Harvard, served a hitch in the Navy, then continued his education at M.I.T. Since the age of thirty-two, he had been engaged in private research, working in his own small laboratory in Riverdale, New York. Plant biology was his field. He published several noteworthy papers, and sold a new insecticide to a development corporation. The royalties helped him to expand his facilities.

Dennison enjoyed working alone. It suited his temperament, which was austere but not unfriendly. Two or three times a year, he would come to New York, see some plays and movies, and do a little serious drinking. He would then return gratefully to his seclusion. He was a bachelor and seemed destined to remain that way.

Not long after his fortieth birthday, Dennison stumbled across an intriguing clue which led him into a different branch of biology. He pursued his clue, developed it, extended it slowly into a hypothesis. After three more years, a lucky accident put the final proofs into his hands.

He had invented a most effective longevity drug. It was not proof against violence; aside from that, however, it could fairly be called an immortality serum.

Now was the time for caution. But years of seclusion had made Dennison unwary of people and their motives. He was more or less heedless of the world around him; it never occurred to him that the world was not equally heedless of him.

He thought only about his serum. It was valuable and patentable. But was it the sort of thing that should be revealed? Was the world ready for an immortality drug?

He had never enjoyed speculation of this sort. But since the atom bomb, many scientists had been forced to look at the ethics of their profession. Dennison looked at his and decided that immortality was inevitable.

Mankind had, throughout its existence, poked and probed into the recesses of nature, trying to figure out how things worked. If one man didn't discover fire, or the use of the lever, or gunpowder, or the atom bomb, or immortality, another would. Man willed to know all nature's secrets, and there was no way of keeping them hidden.

Armed with this bleak but comforting philosophy, Dennison packed his formulas and proofs into a briefcase, slipped a two-ounce bottle of the product into a jacket pocket, and left his Riverdale laboratory. It was already evening. He planned to spend the night in a good midtown hotel, see a movie, and proceed to the Patent Office in Washington the following day.

On the subway, Dennison was absorbed in a newspaper. He was barely conscious of the men sitting on either side of him. He became aware of them only when the man on his right poked him firmly in the ribs.

Dennison glanced over and saw the snub nose of a small automatic, concealed from the rest of the car by a newspaper, resting against his side.

"What is this?" Dennison asked.

"Hand it over," the man said.

Dennison was stunned. How could anyone have known about his discovery? And how could they dare try to rob him in a public subway car?

Then he realized that they were probably just after his money.

"I don't have much on me," Dennison said hoarsely, reaching for his wallet.

The man on his left leaned over and slapped the briefcase. "Not money," he said. "The immortality stuff."

In some unaccountable fashion, they knew. What if he refused to give up his briefcase? Would they dare fire the automatic in the subway? It was a very small caliber weapon. Its noise might not even be heard above the subway's roar. And probably they felt justified in taking the risk for a prize as great as the one Dennison carried.

He looked at them quickly. They were mild-looking men, quietly, almost somberly dressed. Something about their clothing jogged Dennison's memory unpleasantly, but he didn't have time to place the recollection. The automatic was digging painfully into his ribs.

The subway was coming to a station. Dennison glanced at the man on his left and caught the glint of light on a tiny hypodermic.

Many inventors, involved only in their own thoughts, are slow of reaction. But Dennison had been a gunnery officer in the Navy and had seen his share of action. He was damned if he was going to give up his invention so easily.

He jumped from his seat and the hypo passed through the sleeve of his coat, just missing his arm. He swung the briefcase at the man with the automatic, catching him across the forehead with the metal edge. As the doors opened, he ran past a popeyed subway guard, up the stairs and into the street.

The two men followed, one of them streaming blood from his forehead. Dennison ran, looking wildly around for a policeman.

The men behind him were screaming, "Stop, thief! Police! Police! Stop that man!"

Apparently they were also prepared to face the police and to claim the briefcase and bottle as their own. Ridiculous! Yet the complete and indignant confidence in their shrill voices unnerved Dennison. He hated a scene.

Still, a policeman would be best. The briefcase was filled with proof of who he was. Even his name was initialed on the outside of the briefcase. One glance would tell anyone ...

He caught a flash of metal from his briefcase, and, still running, looked at it. He was shocked to see a metal plate fixed to the cowhide, over the place where his initials had been. The man on his left must have done that when he slapped the briefcase.

Dennison dug at the plate with his fingertips, but it would not come off.

It read, *Property of Edward James Flaherty, Smithfield Institute.*

Perhaps a policeman wouldn't be so much help, after all.

But the problem was academic, for Dennison saw no policeman along the crowded Bronx street. People stood aside as he ran past, staring open-mouthed, offering neither assistance nor interference. But the men behind him were still screaming, "Stop the thief! Stop the thief!"

The entire long block was alerted. The people, like some sluggish beast goaded reluctantly into action, began to make tentative movements toward Dennison, impelled by the outraged cries of his pursuers.

Unless he balanced the scales of public opinion, some do-gooder was going to interfere soon. Dennison conquered his shyness and pride, and called out, "Help me! They're trying to rob me! Stop them!"

But his voice lacked the moral indignation, the absolute conviction of his two shrill-voiced pursuers. A burly young man stepped forward to block Dennison's way, but at the last moment a woman pulled him back.

"Don't get into trouble, Charley."

"Why don't someone call a cop?"

"Yeah, where are the cops?"

"Over at a big fire on 178th Street, I hear."

"We oughta stop that guy."

"I'm willing if you're willing."

Dennison's way was suddenly blocked by four grinning youths, teenagers in black motorcycle jackets and boots, excited by the chance for a little action, delighted at the opportunity to hit someone in the name of law and order.

Dennison saw them, swerved suddenly and sprinted across the street. A bus loomed in front of him.

He hurled himself out of its way, fell, got up again and ran on.

His pursuers were delayed by the dense flow of traffic. Their high-pitched cries faded as Dennison turned into a side street, ran down its length, then down another.

He was in a section of massive apartment buildings. His lungs felt like a blast furnace and his left side seemed to be sewed together with red-hot wire. There was no help for it, he had to rest.

It was then that the first bullet, fired from a silenced weapon, chipped a granite wall not three inches from his head. That was when Dennison realized the full extent of his carelessness.

He pulled the bottle out of his pocket. He had hoped to carry out more experiments on the serum before trying it on human beings. Now there was no choice.

Dennison yanked out the stopper and drained the contents.

Immediately he was running again, as a second bullet scored the granite wall. The great blocks of apartments loomed endlessly ahead of him, silent and alien. There were no walkers upon the streets. There was only Dennison, running more slowly now past the immense, blank-faced apartments.

A long black car came up behind him, its searchlight probing into doors and alleys. Was it the police?

"That's him!" cried the shrill, unnerving voice of one of Dennison's pursuers.

Dennison ducked into a narrow alley between buildings, raced down it and into the next street.

There were two cars on that street, at either end of the block, their headlights shining toward each other, moving slowly to trap him in the middle. The alley gleamed with light now, from the first car's headlights shining down it. He was surrounded.

Dennison raced to the nearest apartment building and yanked at the door. It was locked. The two cars were almost even with him. And, looking at them, Dennison remembered the unpleasant jog his memory had given him earlier.

The two cars were hearses.

The men in the subway, with their solemn faces, solemn clothing, subdued neckties, shrill, indignant voices—they had reminded him of undertakers. They had been undertakers!

Of course! Of course! Oil companies might want to block the invention of a cheap new fuel which could put them out of business; steel corporations might try to stop the development of an inexpensive, stronger-than-steel plastic ...

And the production of an immortality serum would put the undertakers out of business.

His progress, and the progress of thousands of other researchers in biology, must have been watched. And when he made his discovery, they had been ready.

The hearses stopped, and somber-faced, respectable-looking men in black suits and pearl-gray neckties poured out and seized him. The briefcase was yanked out of his hand. He felt the prick of a needle in his shoulder. Then, with no transitional dizziness, he passed out.

He came to sitting in an armchair. There were armed men on either side of him. In front of him stood a small, plump, undistinguished-looking man in sedate clothing.

"My name is Mr. Bennet," the plump man said. "I wish to beg your forgiveness, Mr. Dennison, for the violence to which you were subjected. We found out about your invention only at the last moment and therefore had to improvise. The bullets were meant only to frighten and delay you. Murder was not our intention."

"You merely wanted to steal my discovery," Dennison said.

"Not at all," Mr. Bennet told him. "The secret of immortality has been in our possession for quite some time."

"I see. Then you want to keep immortality from the public in order to safeguard your damned undertaking business!"

"Isn't that rather a naive view?" Mr. Bennet asked, smiling. "As it happens, my associates and I are not undertakers. We took on the disguise in order to present an understandable motive if our plan to capture you had misfired. In that event, others would have believed exactly—and only—what you thought: that our purpose was to safeguard our business."

Dennison frowned and watchfully waited.

"Disguises come easily to us," Mr. Bennet said, still smiling. "Perhaps you have heard rumors about a new carburetor suppressed by the gasoline companies, or a new food source concealed by the great food suppliers, or a new synthetic hastily destroyed by the cotton-owning interests. That was us. And the inventions ended up here."

"You're trying to impress me," Dennison said.

"Certainly."

"Why did you stop me from patenting my immortality serum?"

"The world is not ready for it yet," said Mr. Bennet.

"It isn't ready for a lot of things," Dennison said. "Why didn't you block the atom bomb?"

"We tried, disguised as mercenary coal and oil interests. But we failed.

However, we have succeeded with a surprising number of things."

"But what's the purpose behind it all?"

"Earth's welfare," Mr. Bennet said promptly. "Consider what would happen if the people were given your veritable immortality serum. The problems of birth rate, food production, living space all would be aggravated. Tensions would mount, war would be imminent—"

"So what?" Dennison challenged. "That's how things are right now, without immortality. Besides, there have been cries of doom about every new invention or discovery. Gunpowder, the printing press, nitroglycerin, the atom bomb, they were all supposed to destroy the race. But mankind has learned how to handle them. It had to! You can't turn back the clock, and you can't un-discover something. If it's there, mankind must deal with it!"

"Yes, in a bumbling, bloody, inefficient fashion," said Mr. Bennet, with an expression of distaste.

"Well, that's how Man is."

"Not if he's properly led," Mr. Bennet said.

"No?"

"Certainly not," said Mr. Bennet. "You see, the immortality serum provides a solution to the problem of political power. Rule by a permanent and enlightened elite is by far the best form of government; infinitely better than the blundering inefficiencies of democratic rule. But throughout history, this elite, whether monarchy, oligarchy, dictatorship or junta, has been unable to perpetuate itself. Leaders die, the followers squabble for power, and chaos is close behind. With immortality, this last flaw would be corrected. There would be no discontinuity of leadership, for the leaders would always be there."

"A permanent dictatorship," Dennison said.

"Yes. A permanent, benevolent rule by small, carefully chosen elite corps, based upon the sole and exclusive possession of immortality. It's historically inevitable. The only question is, who is going to get control first?"

"And you think you are?" Dennison demanded.

"Of course. Our organization is still small, but absolutely solid. It is bolstered by every new invention that comes into our hands and by every scientist who joins our ranks. Our time will come, Dennison! We'd like to have you with us, among the elite."

"You want me to join you?" Dennison asked, bewildered.

"We do. Our organization needs creative scientific minds to help us in our work, to help us save mankind from itself."

"Count me out," Dennison said, his heart beating fast.

"You won't join us?"

"I'd like to see you all hanged."

Mr. Bennet nodded thoughtfully and pursed his small lips. "You have taken your own serum, have you not?"

Dennison nodded. "I suppose that means you kill me now?"

"We don't kill," Mr. Bennet said. "We merely wait. I think you are a reasonable man, and I think you'll come to see things our way. We'll be around a long time. So will you. Take him away."

Dennison was led to an elevator that dropped deep into the Earth. He was marched down a long passageway lined with armed men. They went through four massive doors. At the fifth, Dennison was pushed inside alone, and the door was locked behind him.

He was in a large, well-furnished apartment. There were perhaps twenty people in the room, and they came forward to meet him.

One of them, a stocky, bearded man, was an old college acquaintance of Dennison's.

"Jim Ferris?"

"That's right," Ferris said. "Welcome to the Immortality Club, Dennison."

"I read you were killed in an air crash last year."

"I merely—disappeared," Ferris said, with a rueful smile, "after inventing the immortality serum. Just like the others."

"All of them?"

"Fifteen of the men here invented the serum independently. The rest are successful inventors in other fields. Our oldest member is Doctor Li, a serum discoverer, who disappeared from San Francisco in 1911. You are our latest acquisition. Our clubhouse is probably the most carefully guarded place on Earth."

Dennison said, "Nineteen-eleven!" Despair flooded him and he sat down heavily in a chair. "Then there's no possibility of rescue?"

"None. There are only four choices available to us," Ferris said. "Some have left us and joined the Undertakers. Others have suicided. A few have gone insane. The rest of us have formed the Immortality Club."

"What for?" Dennison bewilderedly asked.

"To get out of this place!" said Ferris. "To escape and give our discoveries to the world. To stop those hopeful little dictators upstairs."

"They must know what you're planning."

"Of course. But they let us live because, every so often, one of us gives up and joins them. And they don't think we can ever break out. They're much too smug. It's the basic defect of all power-elites, and their eventual undoing."

"You said this was the most closely guarded place on Earth?"

"It is," Ferris said.

"And some of you have been trying to break out for fifty years? Why, it'll take forever to escape!"

"Forever is exactly how long we have," said Ferris. "But we hope it won't take quite that long. Every new man brings new ideas, plans. One of them is bound to work."

"Forever," Dennison said, his face buried in his hands.

"You can go back upstairs and join them," Ferris said, with a hard note to his voice, "or you can suicide, or just sit in a corner and go quietly mad. Take your pick."

Dennison looked up. "I must be honest with you and with myself. I don't think we can escape. Furthermore, I don't think any of you really believe we can."

Ferris shrugged his shoulders.

"Aside from that," Dennison said, "I think it's a damned good idea. If you'll bring me up to date, I'll contribute whatever I can to the Forever Project. And let's hope their complacency lasts."

"It will," Ferris said.

The escape did not take forever, of course. In one hundred and thirty-seven years, Dennison and his colleagues made their successful break-out and revealed the Undertakers' Plot. The Undertakers were tried before the High Court on charges of kidnapping, conspiracy to overthrow the government, and illegal possession of immortality. They were found guilty on all counts and summarily executed.

Dennison and his colleagues were also in illegal possession of immortality, which is the privilege only of our governmental elite. But the death penalty was waived in view of the Immortality Club's service to the State.

This mercy was premature, however. After some months the members of the Immortality Club went into hiding, with the avowed purpose of overthrowing the Elite Rule and disseminating immortality among the masses. Project Forever, as they termed it, has received some support from dissidents, who have not yet been apprehended. It cannot be considered a serious threat.

But this deviationist action in no way detracts from the glory of the Club's escape from the Undertakers. The ingenious way in which Dennison and his colleagues broke out of their seemingly impregnable prison, using only a steel belt buckle, a tungsten filament, three hens' eggs, and twelve chemicals that can be readily obtained from the human body, is too well known to be repeated here.